T5-CCV-943

HELLO . . . NOW DIE!

"Let me introduce myself. My name is Stephen Robinson, and I've come a long way to do two things."

"And what would they be?" Clint asked.

"Well, one of them was meet you," Robinson said.

"And the other?"

"Why, to kill you."

DON'T MISS THESE
ALL-ACTION WESTERN SERIES
FROM THE BERKLEY PUBLISHING GROUP

THE GUNSMITH by J. R. Roberts
Clint Adams was a legend among lawmen, outlaws, and ladies. They called him . . . the Gunsmith.

LONGARM by Tabor Evans
The popular long-running series about U.S. Deputy Marshal Long—his life, his loves, his fight for justice.

LONE STAR by Wesley Ellis
The blazing adventures of Jessica Starbuck and the martial arts master, Ki. Over eight million copies in print.

SLOCUM by Jake Logan
Today's longest-running action Western. John Slocum rides a deadly trail of hot blood and cold steel.

THE GUNSMITH

156

DAKOTA GUNS

J. R. ROBERTS

JOVE BOOKS, NEW YORK

If you purchased this book without a cover, you should be aware that this book is stolen property. It was reported as "unsold and destroyed" to the publisher, and neither the author nor the publisher has received any payment for this "stripped book."

DAKOTA GUNS

A Jove Book / published by arrangement with
the author

PRINTING HISTORY
Jove edition / December 1994

All rights reserved.
Copyright © 1994 by J. R. Roberts.
This book may not be reproduced in whole
or in part, by mimeograph or any other means,
without permission. For information address:
The Berkley Publishing Group, 200 Madison Avenue,
New York, New York 10016.

ISBN: 0-515-11507-X

A JOVE BOOK®
Jove Books are published by The Berkley Publishing Group,
200 Madison Avenue, New York, New York 10016.
JOVE and the "J" design are trademarks
belonging to Jove Publications, Inc.

PRINTED IN THE UNITED STATES OF AMERICA

10 9 8 7 6 5 4 3 2 1

THE GUNSMITH

156

DAKOTA GUNS

PROLOGUE

Stephen Robinson preferred to be called the Canadian Gun. He was thirty years old and had been working very hard over the years to become the fastest gun in Canada. Now that he was, he wanted a name, and he had chosen the Canadian Gun.

To make sure that everyone knew the name, he agreed to an interview with a newspaper from Toronto. He told the writer some stories, some of which were true, most of which were exaggerated, but who was going to tell? The people he exaggerated about were all dead. What did it matter if a couple of them were actually shot in the back? He'd read a lot of penny dreadfuls from the United States about gunmen who made their reputations by shooting men in the back. In some instances he had found it necessary, but that didn't mean he wouldn't have been able to take those men face-to-face if he'd wanted to.

Robinson looked down at the girl who was lying next to him. A lot of women wanted to sleep with him now that he was the Canadian Gun. This one was an eighteen-year-old blonde who worked in her daddy's general store. He had gone in to buy a few items, and she'd recognized him from the newspaper story. When he realized that she knew who he was, he arranged to come back for her after she was finished with work, and then they came here to his hotel room.

In the morning Stephen Robinson would be heading across the border into America. He'd thought about this a lot. Now that he had accomplished what he wanted to in Canada, the next step was to become the fastest gun in the world. (To Stephen Robinson, the world consisted of Canada and the United States—and maybe Mexico.) In order for that to happen, he had to seek out and kill whoever was the fastest gun in America now.

With all the reading he had done about the American West and American gunmen, it was obvious who the fastest gun was—Clint Adams, the Gunsmith.

Robinson knew all about the Gunsmith's reputation, but he also knew that Clint Adams was a lot older than he was. There was no way the man would be able to outdraw him. After all, at thirty Stephen was at his peak. It would be no contest.

All he had to do was find the man.

The blond—whose name he'd forgotten—stirred next to him. He stared down at her.

She was slender and had small breasts, but she had a wonderful ass. He put his hand on it now, rubbing first the right cheek and then the left. She moaned and opened her legs. He slid his hand down between her thighs, found what he wanted, and stroked her with his finger. He knew all about women too, knew what they wanted and how to make them happy.

He slid his finger inside of her, and she gasped and opened her eyes.

He wondered if America—its men and especially its women—were ready for him.

ONE

When Clint Adams rode into North Bend, in the Dakotas, it was with two things in mind. First, he was going to visit with Nelson Fox and his family. Clint had not seen Fox in almost seven years. Nelson and his wife, Carol, had two children. Clint wondered what the Fox's boy Jeff and their daughter Donna would look like now. Jeff had been eight and Donna eleven the last time he'd seen them.

Clint's trips north had not been many. He'd been to Montana several times, and to Canada and Alaska at least once each. He did most of his traveling in either the Southwest or along the West Coast, specifically San Francisco and Sacramento. On occasion he'd gone to Chicago, or New Orleans, or as far east as New York, but he preferred the Southwest.

Nelson and Carol Fox had been writing to Clint at his address in Labyrinth, Texas, for years, inviting him to come up. Nelson promised that the hunting would be superior.

That was the second thing Clint had in mind.
Although he was not much of a hunter these
days, there had been a time when he enjoyed
it. He'd hunted buffalo as a young man in the
company of Wyatt Earp and Bat Masterson,
when the three of them had been trying to
build themselves a stake. He'd also been
involved in hunts for big cats and wolves.
The hunting Nelson Fox had in mind was
deer hunting. The only time Clint had ever
shot deer was for meat, on the trail. Fox, he
knew, hunted it for meat—initially when he
and his family had first settled up north, and
even now, when there were places that meat
could be bought. Fox was the kind of man
who would never spend money for something
he could supply himself.

Clearly, from the constant invitations he had
received from Fox, his friend intended that he
would stay with them at their home. Clint
decided to ride into North Bend first, look the
town over, and register in a hotel. He knew
that even if there was no room for him, Fox
and his family would insist that there was. But
he didn't want to be a burden. He figured that
once he told Nelson Fox that he already had a
room in the hotel, that would be that.

He hoped.

It was cold when Clint arrived in North
Bend. Recent rainstorms and snowstorms had
made a quagmire of the main street. Duke,
his big, black gelding, trod softly for a big
animal, lifting his hooves high. Each time he

did that, though, he tossed mud into the air. Also, they were splattered once or twice by passing wagons.

It was before noon, and North Bend was fairly alive with activity. It looked like a town that was growing, with some new-looking buildings here and there—either newly built or renovated. Main Street had plenty of traffic, including foot traffic. He passed two saloons along the way, but only saw one hotel. Of course, there was no telling what was on the side streets, and North Bend seemed to have a few of those.

By the time they reached the livery, the gelding's coat was liberally covered with brown mud.

The man who came out of the livery was wearing a slicker, like it was still raining, or like he was expecting it. Clint had been lucky up till now. He'd been following along after the rain and had remained dry, albeit a little mud-covered.

"Stayin' long?" the man asked.

"Probably," Clint said. "A week or so, maybe more."

"Visitin'?"

"Yes," Clint said. "The Fox family."

The man nodded.

"Nice people."

He was in his fifties, real thin, about five nine. His hands gave him away as someone who had been working with horses for a long time. They were scarred where he'd been bitten, and the top half of the little finger of his left hand was missing.

"Nice-lookin' animal," he said of Duke.

"He will be," Clint said, "after you've cleaned him off."

"Ornery, is he?"

"Why do you ask?"

"His bearing," the man said. "Appears to be the kind of animal who's particular about who touches him."

"If you're cleaning him and caring for him, he won't bother you," Clint said. "Try to pet him just to pet him and you might lose the other part of that finger."

The man looked down at his half pinky.

"Gotcha."

"How many hotels in town?"

"Couple," the man said. "You passed one on Main Street."

"I did."

"That's the biggest," the man said. "Want somethin' smaller, go back two blocks and turn right. Street name is Charleston. So's the hotel, the Charleston Hotel. Small, but it's got a good dining room."

"And the big one?"

"North Bend Hotel," the man said. "Bigger rooms, but the dining room ain't as good. It's got a saloon, though. The other one don't. Your choice."

"Think I'll go for the good dining room," Clint said. "How's the coffee?"

"Black and strong."

Clint nodded.

"You talked me into it."

As Clint turned to walk away, rifle in one hand and bedroll in the other, the man asked, "Anything else I should know about this brute?"

"Just don't get in his way," Clint said, "and you'll get along fine."

"What is he, about nine?"

"Exactly."

"Set in his ways, is he?"

"Very."

"I'll keep that in mind," the man said. "Don't worry about 'im. I know my way around horses."

"I could tell," Clint said. "I'm not worried. You want some money in advance?"

"Why?" the man asked, looking unconcerned. "I got your horse, don't I?"

"Yeah," Clint said, "you do."

TWO

Clint negotiated the mud from the livery to the side of the street he wanted. When he stepped up on the boardwalk, he banged his feet to knock off some of the excess mud. He knew that later he'd have to clean his boots, either as soon as he got into his room or after the mud dried. Then again, they were the only pair he had, and when he left the hotel they were just going to get muddy again.

Decisions, decisions.

On the way to the hotel he passed a window with some boots in them, and on the spur of the moment he went inside to buy a second pair.

As he entered, the smell of leather floated into his nostrils, along with something else— the smell of perfume, something that smelled strongly of . . . vanilla.

He put his rifle and bedroll down by the door and started looking at some of the boots. There was no one behind the counter at the moment, but presently a woman stepped through a curtained doorway. He stood and stared.

She was blond, probably in her twenties, and extremely attractive. Her hair was long, hanging past her shoulders, and her skin was pale and smooth. She was tall and seemed slender, except for the thrust of her bosom. Standing behind the counter she matched his gaze for a moment before speaking.

"Can I help you?"

"Yes, I, uh, just got to town and I'm interested in a second pair of boots."

"Smart man," she said with a smile. "Our streets will be like this for some time. A second pair of boots is a wise investment."

"I figured."

She came around the counter, and he saw that she was wearing a black skirt and boots to go with the powder-blue shirt. As she got closer, he could see that in her boots she was at least five eleven. The closer she got, the stronger the odor of vanilla got.

"I guess you'd want a fairly inexpensive pair," she said.

"Since I'll be wearing them in the mud, yes."

"Where are you from?"

"Lately, from Texas."

"Not much mud down that way?"

"We get some," he said, "but nothing like this."

"What size do you take?"

"Eleven."

She picked a pair of black boots off one of the shelves and held them out to him.

"Not too expensive, but well made. They'll last you. How long will you be staying in North Bend?"

"A week or more."

"Business?"

"Visiting."

"Oh?"

"The Fox family."

She smiled.

"Really?"

"Yes, why?"

"Oh, I'm just ever so fond of them," she said. "Carol is the sweetest thing, and their daughter Donna and I—well, I see a lot of Donna."

"Well, there's not much of an age difference, is there?"

"Oh, enough," she said with a laugh. "I'm not old enough to be her mother, if that's what you mean, but certainly an older sister. In fact, I think that's the way Donna sees me. When was the last time you saw them?"

"About seven years ago," he said. "Jeff was about eight and I guess Donna was—what? Eleven?"

"Yes," she said, "that would be about right. She's eighteen now."

"My name's Clint Adams," he said.

She stuck out her hand and said, "Brenda Tyler."

He took her hand and said, "A pleasure, Miss Tyler. I'll take these boots."

"I'll put them in a box for you," she said.

He followed her to the counter.

"Will you be going out to see them soon?" she asked. "The Foxes, I mean."

"Pretty soon," he said. "I just got to town, so I'd like to get a meal and freshen up."

"Where will you be staying?"

"Fella at the livery suggested the Charleston," Clint said. "He likes their dining room."

"They do have excellent food there," she said, "and it's not on a busy street."

"Sounds perfect."

She wrapped the boots and put them in a box, and he paid her.

"Well, thanks for your help," he said when he had the box tucked under his left arm.

"Maybe I'll see you at the Fox house," she said. "I'm there fairly often."

"I'll look forward to it, Miss Tyler."

"Oh, Brenda, please," she said. "After all, we do have friends in common, don't we?"

"Yes," he said, "that we do. I hope to see you soon, then."

"Yes," she said, "so do I."

"Good-bye."

"Bye."

He picked up his rifle and bedroll and went outside, thinking that his stay in North Bend might be even more pleasant than he'd first thought.

THREE

Clint found the room at the Charleston Hotel to be more than satisfactory. It was no smaller than any room he'd stayed in at other hotels, which led him to wonder about the size of the rooms in the North Bend Hotel.

He used the pitcher and basin in his room to wash some of the mud from his face and hands. First, though, he cleaned as much mud from his boots as he could, and then pulled on the new pair. They were stiff, but they'd be broken in by tomorrow.

After he was cleaned up, he went down to the dining room to see for himself how good the food was. As it turned out, not only was the coffee to his liking, but the beef stew—a dish he used to judge all restaurants by—was excellent.

After his lunch he pronounced himself very happy with the Charleston Hotel and went out to take a stroll around town.

•   •   •

Clint cut his tour of the town short when he realized how much mud he'd have to deal with. He decided to accept the fact that it was a growing town and as such probably had all the amenities that growing towns had.

During his shortened tour he had seen not only the saloon that was attached to the North Bend Hotel, but another called the Cactus Hall. He decided to go inside and check out the Hall.

From the looks of it, inside and out, the Cactus Hall was a fairly new addition to the town of North Bend. The front facade and the windows were practically free of soot, which was a dead giveaway, and when he got inside, the place still had a new wood smell to it. Even the sawdust on the floor looked fresh.

This early in the day it wasn't doing a booming business. Some of the tables were covered, and Clint had no doubt that these were gaming tables. So the Cactus Hall was also a gambling establishment. That was useful information for someone who spent a good deal of his time gambling—when he had the time.

Actually, Clint's game was poker, and he only indulged in other forms of gambling like blackjack or roulette when a poker game was not available.

He walked up to the bar, which was polished so highly that it gleamed, and waited for the bartender with the bow tie to come down and ask him what he wanted.

"Beer."

"Comin' up."

The man was not only dressed in a shirt and tie, but his hair was slicked down and he smelled of bay rum.

Clint looked around and saw only a handful of men in the place. Two of them were seated together at a table, a third was sitting alone, and a fourth was standing at the other end of the bar. He'd been talking with the bartender when Clint walked in. Clint saw the bartender go back to the man and say something before he drew his beer and carried it back to him.

"There you go," the bartender said, and Clint thought he detected a bit of nervousness in the man.

"Thanks."

He didn't watch the bartender, but the man at the end of the bar. Up till now the man's body had been facing the bar, but he turned and Clint saw the badge on his shirt. That explained things. The bartender had recognized him and had told the sheriff.

The sheriff pushed away from the bar, leaving his beer half finished, and walked over to where Clint was standing, facing the bar now and sipping his drink.

"Clint Adams, isn't it?"

Clint looked at the lawman. He was about thirty-five, with dark black sideburns and mustache. Clint assumed that the hair beneath the hat would also be black. He studied the man's eyes for a moment and detected no fear or nervousness, only curiosity.

"That's right."

"My name's Jack Grady, Adams," the man said. "I'm the sheriff here in North Bend."

"I can see that."

"Just get into town?"

"That's right."

"Plan on staying long?"

"Long enough to visit with some friends."

"Friends? Who might that be?"

"Nelson Fox and his family."

The sheriff nodded.

"How long have you known Nelson Fox?"

"A lot of years."

"Been long since you seen him?"

"About seven years."

"You plan on staying out at his place or here in town?"

"Sheriff, I've taken a room at the Charleston Hotel for now. I don't know what I'll be doing once I talk to Nelson. If there's something specific you'd like to ask me, why don't you get to it?"

"I'm just doin' my job, Adams."

"You're pussyfooting around me, Sheriff, and that makes me uncomfortable. You want to know if I'm here looking for trouble? The answer's no. You want to know if I'll run away from trouble if it comes looking for me? The answer's no. Anything else?"

"I just don't want anybody getting any ideas, Adams," the lawman said. "Man with your reputation comes to town, people get ideas."

"Hotheads, you mean."

"Yes."

"Men—or boys—who want to try me out."

"That's right."

"You got anybody in town like that, Sheriff?"

"Not that I know of."

"Then what are you worried about?"

"I said, not that I know of," Grady said. "I don't know everyone in town. I don't know what's goin' on in everybody's mind."

"Then I think you should be watching your townspeople, Sheriff, and not me."

"It'll be a lot easier on me, Adams, to watch you."

Clint studied the man for a moment. He had started out dancing around the issue, but now he wasn't backing off a step.

"I guess it would at that, Sheriff," Clint said. "Why don't we start over and let me buy you a fresh beer? The one you left down there looks a little flat from here."

The sheriff thought a moment, then said, "Sure, why not?"

Clint waved at the bartender, who brought another beer over, set it down nervously, and hurried back to the other end of the bar.

FOUR

Once they stopped playing games with each other, Clint and Sheriff Grady got along fine. They had a beer together, and Clint found out from Grady that he had been sheriff for about three years. Coincidentally, that was when the town started growing. An influx of new blood, new ranchers, even some mining activity, was the cause.

"Must make your job interesting," Clint said, "an active town like this."

"It has its moments," Grady admitted.

After the first beer Grady turned around and bought Clint one. While they were talking more and more people came into the saloon, and finally the covers were removed from some of the gaming tables.

"I've got to get going," Grady said. "I got a job to do, if I remember right."

"Sure."

"Listen," he said before leaving, "I'm sorry if I came on too strong. When you only know

19

somebody by their reputation . . ."

"It's okay," Clint said, "I understand."

"The Foxes are a nice family," Grady said. "Give my best to Donna—I mean, to all of them."

"I will. I think I'll ride out there now, before it gets much later."

"Are they expecting you today?"

"Expecting me is about it," Clint said. "They don't know when I'll be arriving."

"Then it'll be a nice surprise, won't it?"

"That it will."

As the sheriff went out, Clint finished his beer and once again went over the ages of the Fox kids in his head. He felt sure he had Jeff's age right. The boy would be fifteen now. He was thinking about Donna's age, though. She couldn't be more than eighteen, and yet the sheriff—all of thirty-five if he was a day—certainly seemed sweet on her.

Well, Donna had been a pretty little girl, and if she'd grown up to look anything like her mother he could understand the sheriff going sweet on her.

He looked around. The gambling was starting, and if he got involved in it he'd never get out to the Fox ranch. As it was, he'd probably get there just in time for a good, hot, home-cooked dinner.

Nobody ever said his timing was bad.

When Clint reclaimed Duke from the livery stable, the gelding was as clean as he could be. He also looked pretty happy, which meant he was probably being treated more than right.

"Gonna take him out and get him all muddy again?" the liveryman asked.

"I'm afraid so," Clint said. "Time to go out and see Nelson and his family. I'll probably get as muddy as him, though."

"Well, you tell 'em Rufus down to the livery says hey, you hear?"

"I'll tell them," Clint said, mounting up. "He feels nice and relaxed."

"Yeah, well, I told you, I know horses. I been takin' care of him."

"And I'm much obliged for it, Rufus," Clint said. "See you later."

"You get in late, you come over to the boardinghouse where I live," the liveryman said, "and I'll take him in for you, get him cleaned up again."

"Thanks, Rufus," Clint said. "I'll do that."

FIVE

Clint had never seen the place Nelson Fox had fixed up for him and his family. The last time Clint saw them, Nelson and Carol and the kids were leaving Texas and heading north. As Clint rode up to the place, he was impressed. He'd certainly seen larger spreads over the years, but this one was tidy, just exactly what Nelson Fox said he always wanted.

The house was one story but looked large enough to accommodate the four of them comfortably. There was a corral with about ten or twelve good-looking horses in it. Fox had always said he wanted to raise the finest horses in the country, and it didn't look like he'd missed by much.

As Clint rode up to the corral, a boy came out of the barn. He was carrying a bucket of something and stopped short when he saw the man on the big, black horse.

The boy was tall with broad shoulders but not filled out yet, so he looked bony. His hair was curly black, like his father's, and his eyes were wide as he studied the big, black gelding's lines.

"Jeez, mister," he said, putting the bucket down, "that's the biggest horse I ever seen."

Clint dismounted and said, "Come and take a closer look, son."

Jeff Fox came closer, and Clint saw that the boy was almost six feet tall. He found this odd, since Nelson Fox was barely five nine and his wife was about five three. Where had the boy got his height from?

The boy looked Duke over and said, "What is he, about nine?"

"Right on the button," Clint said. "You know your horses."

"I know almost as much about 'em as Pa does," Jeff said proudly.

"I'll bet he's real proud of you."

Jeff didn't reply. He was still too interested in looking at Duke, his eyes very wide.

"He's so beautiful," Jeff said. "Can I touch him?"

"I wouldn't recommend it, son," Clint said. "At least, not until he knows you a little better."

Jeff moved his hand, as if sorely tempted to touch the big black, but then he drew it away.

"Is your pa home, Jeff?"

The boy turned his eyes from Duke to Clint and asked, "How do you know my name—" Then he stopped short, as if something had just occurred to him. "Wait a minute."

He looked at Duke again, and then at Clint, working something over in his head.

"You're Clint Adams, ain't you?" he finally asked.

"That's right, Jeff."

"Oh," the boy said. "Oh, I shoulda knowed when I saw the horse. Pa talks about you and your horse all the time."

"Well, the last time your pa saw Duke he was a lot younger," Clint said, "but then so were me and your pa. Is he home?"

"He sure is, Mr. Adams," the boy said anxiously, "and Ma, too. They're up at the house. Come on, I'll take you there."

"You lead the way, son."

"Well, come on," Jeff said again, and started for the house.

Clint followed the boy, who was trying to contain himself and not run up to the house. He was walking ahead of Clint, who led Duke behind him. When they reached the house, Clint dropped Duke's reins and watched as the boy burst through the door.

"He's here!" he heard the boy shout. "Clint Adams is here!"

SIX

Nelson Fox came running out of his house and started pumping Clint's hand madly. Clint was shocked into silence by Fox's appearance. The last time he'd seen the man, he'd been slender, probably weighing no more than 160 pounds. The man who was shaking his hand now weighed at least a hundred pounds more than that, most of it around the middle.

Behind Fox came his wife, Carol. Always as pretty as could be, Carol Fox had not changed in seven years. In fact, she was even lovelier than she'd been the last time he'd seen her, if that was possible. She had dark hair that was pinned up, with some loose strands flying around. She was wearing a plain dress that did absolutely nothing for her, but she did wonders for it.

"Clint," she said warmly, and got up on her toes to kiss his cheek while her husband continued to pump his hand.

"Hello, Carol," he said. "You're prettier than ever, I see."

"Oh, you . . ." she said.

Jeff came out of the house and was watching the reunion. Clint did not see Donna anywhere.

"Where's Donna?"

He saw a glance pass between husband and wife, and then Carol said, "Oh, she'll be back soon. It's almost supper time."

"You old horse thief," Nelson Fox said, finally releasing Clint's hand. "You really came."

"Yeah, Nels, I really came," Clint said. "Didn't you think I would?"

"Well, after seven years of 'maybe next year' what would make me think any different about this year?"

"I see your point," Clint said sheepishly.

"Never mind that," Carol said, taking hold of Clint's arm, "he's here now, and that's what's important. Come inside, Clint."

"I've got a bottle of whiskey I've been waiting for a special occasion to open," Nelson said. "By golly, I think this is it."

"Can I have a drink?" Jeff asked.

The three adults looked over at him.

He shrugged and said, "I mean, it is a special occasion, ain't it?"

Clint saw Carol looking at her husband, but Nelson never looked over at her.

"Sure," he said, "why not? One little drink isn't gonna hurt anything."

He turned to Clint and said, "Come on inside, Clint. Jeff, you can have that drink after you take care of Clint's horse."

"Can I?" Jeff asked.

"Oh, I can do that—" Clint started dubiously, only to be interrupted by Nelson Fox.

"Let him do it, Clint," he said. "The boy knows how to handle a horse."

"Yes, Nels, but Duke—"

Nelson looked over at the big gelding and shook his head admiringly.

"He sure has filled out, ain't he?"

"He has, and he's a little ornery at times."

"Jeff can handle an ornery horse, Clint," Nelson said. "Give him a chance, will you?"

Clint walked over to Duke and patted his neck. The big gelding tossed his head.

"All right," Clint said, taking up the gelding's reins and holding them out, "he's all yours, Jeff."

Jeff bounded off the porch, then slowed down as he approached Duke. He accepted the reins from Clint as if they were gold.

"I'll take real good care of him, Mr. Adams."

"It's Clint," he said, "and I know you will, son. I'll see you inside."

"Come on, Clint," Carol said, gripping his arm impatiently, "I want to show you the inside of the house."

SEVEN

When Clint entered the house he could see why Carol Fox was so anxious to show it to him. Nelson Fox had built the house himself, and Clint knew Nelson well enough to know that it had been constructed soundly. What he had not expected was that Carol Fox could have been such a gifted decorator.

He didn't know much about decorating houses, but what he saw impressed him. The rugs, the curtains, even the cloth on the table all matched or complemented each other, as did the furniture, all of which looked store-bought and expensive.

"When we first moved in," she explained, "all we had was the furniture Nelson had built."

"And damned good furniture it was too," Nelson added indignantly.

"It was good furniture," Carol said, "I'm not saying it wasn't, but I wanted real, store-bought furniture like I'd been seeing in catalogues for years."

They were sitting at the kitchen table. Nelson and Clint each had a glass of whiskey, while Carol had made herself a cup of tea. They had showed Clint the house, which had six rooms. Originally, they said, it had four, but after the first two years Nelson had added another room, and then three years later the sixth. Now Jeff and Donna actually had their own rooms, which Nelson and Carol had never heard of while they were growing up.

Nelson put his hand on Carol's and said, "I had to get her what she wanted, Clint, so she wouldn't leave me for someone who could."

"Oh, you . . ." she said, pulling her hand away from his. "Don't listen to him, he's talking nonsense."

At that moment the front door opened and Jeff came walking in.

"You still got all your fingers?" Clint asked him.

"Yeah," he said, holding both hands up.

"Well, you were out there long enough," his mother said.

"I wanted to take good care of him," Jeff said. Clint had only heard a few people refer to Duke as "him" the way the boy did. He liked Jeff for it.

"I guess you got a drink coming, then," Clint said.

Carol did not look happy.

"A small drink," Nelson said, sensing his wife's displeasure.

Nelson poured out just enough whiskey to coat the bottom of a shot glass.

"Was your first drink bigger than that, Clint?" the disappointed youngster asked.

"Yes, it was," Clint said, "but I didn't have it until I was seventeen."

"Really?"

"Really."

That seemed to mollify the youth. He picked up his drink and downed it like a man. The next moment he was having a coughing fit and his mother was pounding on his back while Clint and Nelson laughed.

"Are you all right?" Carol asked.

"I—I'm fine, Ma," he said, all but pushing her away, "I'm fine."

She withdrew her hands and looked at him until he had caught his breath.

"Jeff, do me a favor and watch for your sister, all right?"

"Why?" he asked. "It's not like she's alone—"

"Please?"

"All right," he said, shaking his head. He looked at Clint and asked, "Can we talk later?"

"Sure," Clint said.

"After dinner," Carol said.

"Like your mother says, after dinner."

"All right," Jeff said and went outside to watch for his sister.

"Why does he have to watch for her?" Clint asked. "Is there a problem?"

"With an eighteen-year-old girl there's always a problem," Nelson said, but Clint felt that the remark was designed to avoid an actual answer.

"Why don't you both go outside for a sit also?" Carol suggested. "I've got to get dinner on the table."

"Is there enough?" Clint asked. "I know I showed up without notice—"

"We've been expecting you for seven years," Nelson said, slapping Clint on the back. "Don't worry, there's enough food."

EIGHT

Clint and Nelson Fox went out onto the porch, where Jeff was sitting on the second of the two steps. The boy had his hand to his mouth when they came out and quickly moved it away. Probably trying to wipe away the taste of the whiskey.

"Where is your gear?" Nelson asked as they sat down on a couple of chairs.

"In town."

"You didn't take a hotel room?"

"I did."

"That's nonsense," Nelson said. "You're gonna stay here with us."

"I'm already in the hotel, Nels," he said, "and it's a pretty nice town."

"You're kiddin'!" Nelson said. "It's a mud hole and you know it. Come out here. What good is having your own place if you can't share it with friends?"

Clint looked over Nelson Fox's spread.

"You work this place yourself, Nels?" he asked.

32

"I help," Jeff said, turning around quickly.

"Jeff . . ." Nelson said.

"What?"

"Clint and I are trying to talk."

"I know you help, Jeff," Clint said. "I assumed that. I meant is there anyone else?"

"I have some hands, and a top hand," Nelson said. "He breaks my horses for me."

"No foreman?"

"I don't need a foreman," Nelson said. "It's not a big operation, Clint, it's just big enough for us."

"I didn't see a bunkhouse."

"There's a small one out behind the house," Nelson said, "but only Will Cord, my top hand, stays there. The others come to work in the morning and leave in the evening."

Nelson chose that moment to sit up straight and look around.

"I don't see Donna," he said. "Jeff, take a walk and see if you can spot your sister."

Jeff turned and looked at his father. He wondered if he should tell that he already knew where his sister was, but then he decided against it.

"I'll take a walk," he said, and got up and did so.

"Is there a real problem with Donna?" Clint asked when Jeff was gone.

For a moment Clint thought he was going to get the "she's eighteen" story again, but then Nelson closed his mouth and thought a moment.

"I don't know what she does or where she goes, Clint," he said. "I guess that qualifies as a problem."

"She is eighteen, though," Clint said. "She's not a kid anymore."

"Maybe not, but she lives here and I'd like to know what's going on in her life. She's . . . she's a beautiful kid, Clint, and men are always after her."

Clint remembered the look in the sheriff's eyes when he talked about her and understood what Nelson must have been feeling—as much as he could, having no children of his own.

"I don't want her gettin' pregnant," Nelson said. "Not before she's married, anyway."

"Is there someone she wants to marry?"

"That's just it," Nelson said. "There are lots of men, but nobody she wants to marry. That's my problem."

Clint frowned, sincerely happy that it wasn't a problem he'd ever have.

NINE

Will Cord looked down at Donna Fox, who was lying with him on his bed in the bunk-house.

"You know," he said, "if your pa ever hires any other full-time hands, we won't be able to do this anymore."

He ran his hand over her flat bare belly as he spoke.

"We'd just find another place," she said, rubbing his arm.

Cord marveled at her beauty. Her long brown hair that fell around her shoulders and firm breasts. She was slender, with almost no hips, but he knew that she would fill in as she got older.

Cord was twenty-seven and had been working for Nelson Fox for seven months. This was the longest he had ever stayed at a job, and Donna Fox was the main reason. He knew she was in love with him, and he was almost ready to admit that he was in love with her, but he wasn't ready to get married, and that's what he knew she'd want if he admitted it. So, he had to wait, and so did she.

"Isn't it gettin' near dinnertime?" he asked.

"Is it?" she asked. "Kiss me, Will."

He leaned down and kissed her, easily at first, and then with more fervor as she demanded it. Suddenly there were three quick knocks on the door.

"Jesus!" Cord said, jerking his head up.

"Take it easy," she said. "It's just my brother warning me that Pa's lookin' for me."

"Scared the shit out of me," Cord said.

"You ain't afraid of my pa, are you, Will?"

"Not afraid of him, no," he said, "but afraid he'd fire me, and then I wouldn't get to see you again."

"You're sweet," she said. "Kiss me again?"

"Donna, he's lookin' for you—"

"Kiss me again, and then I'll leave."

"Promise?"

"I promise."

He kissed her again and abruptly she wrapped her arms and legs around him, holding him tightly to him. She could feel his hard erection trapped between them.

"Donna—"

"I love you, Will."

"Donna," Cord said, "you have to go."

She stared at his face for a few moments, and when she was convinced that he wasn't going to tell her he loved her she said, "I know," and swung her feet to the floor.

Cord watched her dress, amazed at how much he enjoyed it. She moved like a young, unbroken filly—in bed and out. Cord was used to being with older women and had been surprised to discover that he liked being with the eighteen-year-old Donna Fox.

He'd worked there a few months, saying nothing more than good morning or good afternoon to her, and then one day she showed up at the door of the bunkhouse and said, "I think it's time to stop the crap."

He'd stood there, stunned, while she'd shucked off her clothes and then started to undress him.

"I can do that," he'd said, pushing her hands away.

"Then what are you waiting for?"

"I—I like to do the asking." He'd been completely thrown off balance by her bold behavior.

She had taken a step back, cocked her hip, and placed her hand on it.

"So . . . ask."

He did, and they'd been meeting in the bunkhouse ever since.

Now she sat down next to him on the cot and pulled her boots on.

"I don't know if I'll be able to come tomorrow," she said.

"Why not?"

"We're expecting a guest," she said.

"Clint Adams?"

"My father told you?"

"Yeah, but he also said he wouldn't be surprised if he didn't show up."

"Well, if they're looking for me now, my hunch is he showed up today."

"Why does that mean you won't be able to come?"

She stood up and said, "It might be harder to sneak away. I just have to see how things go, Will."

She started for the door and he called out, "Donna."

He got up and walked naked to her, took her in his arms, and kissed her.

"I . . ." he said, but he let his voice trail off before he finished the sentence. A damned three word sentence and he couldn't get it out.

She touched a hand to his cheek and said, "I have to go, Will."

He stood there and watched her go out the door, then moved to the window and watched her walk around the side of the house and out of sight.

He turned and walked back to the cot, picked up his clothes and started to dress. In all the months Will had worked there Nelson Fox had never invited him into the house to eat. Not even for a cup of coffee. Then again, why should he? After all, Will was just a hired hand. Would that change, though, if Fox found out about him and Donna? That is, if he and Donna got married?

What would Nelson Fox do then?

Fully dressed, he walked to the barn to saddle his horse. He was going to go into town for dinner, and then a few drinks and maybe some poker.

In the barn he saw the big, black gelding in one of the stalls and knew that Donna's hunch was right. The Gunsmith had arrived. He'd have a little news to spread in town over a beer or two.

TEN

Clint was still sitting out front with Nelson Fox when Jeff came back into view.

"Did you find her?" Nelson asked.

"I did," Jeff said, sitting down on the top step. "She's comin'."

"Where was she?"

Jeff shrugged and didn't look at his father.

"You found her, you must know where she was," Nelson said.

"Ask her."

"Jeff—"

"Ask *her*, I said," Jeff snapped, turning only halfway to his father. He was still not making eye contact, which to Clint's way of thinking was a dead giveaway that he was hiding something.

Clint saw Nelson toss a glance his way. He had a feeling that the man would have pursued the matter if he hadn't been there.

At that moment a girl came walking around from the other side of the house and Clint found himself staring, stunned. Even with her father's comment about her looks and the sheriff's remarks, Clint had not expected this stunning young woman who was approaching the porch.

"Clint?" she said. "Is that you?"

Clint stood up as she mounted the porch and gave him a hug—a disconcerting hug. He hesitated to put his arms around her, but when he did she pressed herself against him and he felt her breasts against his chest.

He held her at arm's length and said, "I think that should be my question. My God, girl, but you grew up . . . gorgeous."

"Oh, you . . ." she said, which indicated that to some degree she took after her mother.

Clint looked at Nelson and asked, "What have you been feeding this girl?"

"I'm not a girl anymore, Clint," she said, putting her hands on her hips, "I'm a woman."

"I can see that."

"We've been waiting on dinner for you, Donna," Nelson said.

"Well, I'm here," Donna said. "Let's go inside and eat."

She slipped her arm through Clint's and turned him toward the door. He saw her throw a glance over her shoulder at her brother but was not in position to see if Jeff was returning it.

He was dead sure that brother and sister shared a secret.

• • •

Donna helped Carol get the table set up with food, and then they all sat down to dinner. Clint couldn't help but feel the tension at the table. There was tension between Nelson and Jeff, Nelson and Donna, Carol and Donna, and even some between Nelson and Carol. The only place he didn't sense tension was between brother and sister. There was a bond there and a shared secret. The boy was definitely covering up for his older sister.

But covering up what?

ELEVEN

When Will Cord got to town, he went directly to the Cactus Hall Saloon. Even though it was crowded, he was able to find a table to sit at. Much of the crowd was bellied up to the gaming tables, losing money at baccarat or roulette or faro.

The Cactus Hall served simple meals like steak and eggs and such, and that was good enough for Will Cord.

Sally, one of the saloon girls, came over when she saw him. When he'd first arrived in North Bend he'd spent some time in Sally's bed, but all that had ended when he took up with Donna Fox.

"Hello, Will."

"Hi, Sally."

"You wantin' to eat?"

"Yes. I'll have steak and fixin's."

"Sure. Uh, you plannin' to stay on awhile after you eat tonight?"

"Maybe, Sally," he said.

"Well . . . I'll get your food for you."

"Thanks."

"Want something to drink while you're waitin'?"

"Yeah, a beer should do it."

"Comin' up."

He watched her walk away. She was blond and pretty and close to his own age, but he couldn't help comparing her to Donna, and Sally always came away second best.

She gave his order to the bartender and then brought a beer to his table.

"So what's new with you?" she asked. "Haven't seen you for a few days."

"They're keepin' me busy out at the ranch," he said.

"I bet."

He looked at Sally and wondered if she suspected that something was going on between him and Donna. He'd been real careful to keep that fact to himself and he assumed that Donna was doing the same.

"There is some news, though."

"Oh? Like what?"

He took a swallow of beer before continuing.

"There's a guest out at the house."

"Who?"

"A famous man."

Her eyes widened.

"Really? Come on, tell me who."

"Clint Adams," Cord told her.

She frowned.

"He's famous? I don't know him."

"Maybe you know him by his other name," Cord said. "The Gunsmith."

Her eyes widened even more.

"Really? The Gunsmith? What's he doin' out there?"

"Seems him and Nelson Fox are old friends," Cord explained.

"Is he stayin' for a while?"

"Probably."

"Golly," she said, "I gotta tell the girls. He's real famous, ain't he?"

"He sure is," Cord said.

"Wow." Sally hurried away to spread the news around.

Before long everyone in the saloon knew that the Gunsmith was in town. Now, with quite a few traveling men in the place the news left town with them and spread throughout the county, and within a matter of days it would spread even further than that.

Far enough for someone who was on the lookout for Clint Adams to hear it.

Someone like the man who called himself the Canadian Gun.

TWELVE

During dinner Clint brought up the subject of Brenda Tyler.

"Brenda's great!" Donna said immediately.

"How did you meet Brenda?" Carol asked Clint.

"I needed a second pair of boots, what with all the mud and all, and I went into her place. She helped me pick them out. She said that you and she were good friends," he said to Carol. Then he looked at Donna and added, "And you too."

"Brenda's a good friend of the family," Nelson said. "We should have her out while you're here, Clint. You couldn't do much better than Brenda."

"Nels!" Carol said.

"I would have thought Carol would be the matchmaker in the family, Nelson," Clint said.

"We should do that," Donna said enthusiastically. "Did you like her, Clint?"

46

"Well, we only spoke briefly, Donna—"

"You liked her," Donna said, cutting him off. "I can tell."

"All right," he said, "yes, I liked her."

"I knew it!"

"Well," Carol said, "maybe we'll have her out, then."

For some reason Clint didn't think Carol was quite as enthusiastic about the idea.

After dinner Clint convinced Nelson and Carol Fox that he should go back to town and stay in the hotel that night, since he had not brought any gear with him.

"Well, okay," Nelson said, "but tomorrow morning you get your ass out here, gear and all."

They were on the porch outside, away from Carol and the others, so Clint spoke freely.

"Nelson, I think I can guess that there are some problems out here."

"Problems?" Nelson asked. "What problems?"

Clint studied his friend. Either the man was denying it to himself, or he really didn't see that there were any problems.

"Some personal problems," Clint said. "Like between you and Donna?"

"Oh, that's just Donna—"

"And I thought I detected something between you and Jeff?"

"Jeff . . . is fifteen, Clint—"

"Nelson," Clint said, "you don't have a guest room, and I don't want to put anyone out."

"Clint—"

"Think it over tonight," Clint said. "I'll come back in the afternoon."

"When are we going hunting?" Nelson asked.

"Let's wait a day," Clint said.

"Carol's gonna be real disappointed if you don't stay, Clint."

"Talk to her, Nelson," Clint said, putting his hand on his friend's arm.

"I really don't know what kind of problems you're talking about, Clint," Nelson said, "but all right. We'll see you tomorrow for lunch, all right?"

"I'll be here."

Nelson Fox watched as Jeff brought Duke out of the barn already saddled.

"Thanks, Jeff."

"He's great, Clint," Jeff said, handing him the reins. "Think I could ride him while you're here?"

"I think that's going to be up to Duke, Jeff," Clint said, mounting up. "We'll see, okay?"

"Okay."

"See you tomorrow."

Jeff waved as Clint turned and rode off toward town.

When Clint was gone Jeff turned, saw his father standing on the porch, pushed his hands into his pockets and walked off.

Clint rode off, thinking it ironic that he'd finally got around to visiting his old friend

and seemed to have walked right into a case
of family strife.

At least, he hoped it was only family strife.

Carol came out and saw Jeff walking away.

"Where's he going?" she asked.

"I don't know," Nelson said. "What's Donna
doing?"

"Cleaning up."

"Did you find out where she was?"

"No, Nelson," she said, "I didn't ask
her."

"Carol . . ."

"You couldn't get Clint to stay?"

"No."

"Well, is he going to stay the rest of the time
he's here?"

"I don't know," Nelson said.

"What did he say?"

Nelson looked at his wife.

"He said he could tell we were having some
problems here and he didn't want to get in our
way."

Carol bit her lip, then said, "Well, he's still
perceptive, isn't he?"

"Personal problems, he said," Nelson went
on, "with the kids."

"Then he doesn't know—"

"No," Nelson said, "he doesn't know."

"Nelson," she said, "if he stays in town, he's
sure to hear about it."

"I know," Nelson said. "If it wasn't for the
kids—"

"Don't blame the kids."

"Why not?" he asked. "They're picking the wrong time to become difficult."

"We can't blame them for everything," she said, putting her hand on her husband's arm.

He covered her hand with his and patted it.

"I know we can't," he said, "I know. . . ."

"What are we going to do?"

"I don't know, Carol," Nelson said, looking into the gathering darkness, "I really don't know."

THIRTEEN

The Fox place was less than an hour's ride from town so Clint made it back to North Bend with plenty of time left in the evening. When Clint got to the stable the liveryman, Rufus, was still there and expressed surprise at seeing Clint and Duke back so soon.

"Thought you'd be back later," he said. "Cut your visit short?"

"Just for tonight," Clint said. "I'll probably be going back out tomorrow."

"This big boy will be ready," Rufus said, "don't you worry."

Clint left Duke in the liveryman's capable hands and started back toward the hotel. He changed his mind along the way, though, and made for the Cactus Hall Saloon. He wanted to see what the place was like when it was in full swing.

After he finished his steak, Will Cord gave up his table for a place at the bar. That's where he was standing, working on another beer, when Sheriff Jack Grady walked into the place.

Cord knew that Grady was sweet on Donna Fox, and that Donna kept putting the man off. He didn't think that Grady knew about him and Donna, and yet the sheriff seemed to have it in for him just because he lived behind the Fox house.

Grady stopped just inside the door and surveyed the room. This was one stop on his rounds, but he usually put in a few extra stops as well, both here and at the North Bend Saloon. They were the two places where trouble usually started.

He remained just inside the batwing doors, looking around until his eyes fell on Will Cord, standing at the bar.

Cord tried not to show that he had noticed the man approaching him by turning his back and looking into his beer. He did not want trouble with the law.

Grady moved up behind Cord and waited to see if the bronc buster would notice him. When he didn't, he elbowed his way next to him. The man he elbowed turned to say something, but when he saw Grady's badge he just moved without saying a word.

"Cord," Grady said, just to get the man's attention.

The bronc buster looked at him and said, "Oh, hello, Sheriff."

"How are things out at the Fox place?"

"Fine, Sheriff, just fine."

"Understand they got a visitor out there," Grady said. "Clint Adams."

"That's what I heard."

"Have you met him?"

"Saw his horse in the barn," Cord said. "That's the closest I got to him."

"I met him."

"You did?"

Grady nodded.

"Earlier today. Right in here, as a matter of fact. Seemed like a nice enough fella."

"If you say so."

"Maybe you'll get to meet him too."

"Maybe."

"Haven't seen much of Miss Donna in town lately," Grady said.

"Is that a fact?"

"Yep," Grady said. "They must be keepin' her pretty busy out there too, huh?"

"I guess so."

"Get to see her much?"

"Some."

"I envy you," Grady said. "That's a mighty pretty girl."

"She sure is."

Grady remained silent for a few moments while he caught the eye of the bartender, who brought him a beer. He didn't offer to buy Cord a fresh one.

"Get to talk to her much out there?"

"Some," Cord said. It was the best answer he could come up with. It meant very little.

"Young fella like you," Grady went on, "working out there, I guess you must be pretty sweet on her, huh?"

"She's the boss's daughter, Sheriff," Cord said. "One thing I learned a long time ago is that you don't mess with the boss's daughter."

"Is that a fact?"

"Yeah, it is."

Grady turned to face Cord now, who remained bent over, facing the bar.

"You tryin' to tell me that you work out there and see her every day and you ain't never . . . I mean, you ain't never thought about . . ."

"Oh, sure," Cord said, "I thought about it. . . ."

That seemed to rub the lawman the wrong way, and Cord was immediately sorry he'd said it.

"I think you should stick to your own advice, Cord," the lawman said.

"What's that?"

"Don't mess with the boss's daughter. She ain't gonna look twice at a cowhand."

Now that rubbed Cord the wrong way, and he turned his head to look at Grady.

"Is that so? You think she's gonna bother with a town sheriff?"

"That's better than a cowhand," Grady said. "Ain't it?"

Cord did not want to get into an argument with the lawman, so he just said, "If you say so, Sheriff."

"I do," Grady said, "I say so."

Cord just nodded and sipped his beer.

Grady was going to say something else when the batwing doors opened and Clint Adams stepped in.

"I gotta go," he said to Cord. "Clint Adams just came in."

Interested, Cord took a look over his shoulder.

"That's him, huh?"

"That's him," Grady said, "the legend himself."

"Word's gonna get around fast, Sheriff."

"I know it," Grady said.

"You think there's gonna be trouble?"

"I hope not," Grady said, "I got enough trouble what with everything goin' on between Fox and McFall."

McFall was the other horse breeder in the area and Nelson Fox's competition.

"I better pay a call on Mr. Adams," Grady said leaving his beer. "We'll talk more later."

"We got nothin' to talk about, Sheriff."

"I think we do," Grady said firmly, "but it'll have to be another time."

Cord didn't say anything, he just turned and watched with interest as Grady walked across the room toward the Gunsmith.

FOURTEEN

Clint saw the sheriff coming toward him and knew that the man was about to do his job, again. That meant talking to him and making sure that he didn't intend to kill anyone that night. Maybe he should have gone straight to the hotel after all.

"Evenin', Adams," Sheriff Grady said.

"Hello, Sheriff."

"Back from your visit so soon?"

"For the night, yes," Clint said. "I'll be going back tomorrow for lunch."

"Intending to stay in town, then?"

"Oh, I don't know yet," Clint said. "There's lots of mud, but there seem to be other things that might make up for it."

Grady looked around and said, "Yeah, it gets pretty busy in here, all right."

"Trouble spot, though, right?"

"Well, what with the liquor, and the gamblin', and the girls, if trouble does come up it's usually here, or at the North Bend Saloon."

"Heading over there, are you?"

Grady nodded.

"Making my rounds."

"Well, I won't keep you," Clint said. "I just dropped in for a beer and a look-see."

"Won't be stayin', then?"

"I might," Clint said, "for a while."

That didn't make the sheriff very happy.

"Well, I'll check back here later. Maybe I'll see you then."

"Maybe."

Grady left the saloon and Clint walked over to the bar and took the space the lawman had just vacated. He pushed the sheriff's beer away and waved at the bartender for a fresh one.

"Clint Adams, right?" the man on his right asked.

"That's right," he said. "Do I know you?"

"No," the man said. "My name's Will Cord, Mr. Adams. I work for Mr. Fox."

"Ah," Clint said, remembering, "you're the bronc buster, right?"

"That's me."

They shook hands.

"Can I buy you a fresh beer?" Clint asked, seeing that Cord's beer was almost gone.

"Sure," Cord said. "Much obliged."

Clint called the bartender over and ordered Cord another beer.

"I've heard a lot about you," Clint said to the younger man.

"Well, I think I might have heard a little bit more about you," Cord said.

"From Nelson, you mean?"

"From Mr. Fox, yes," Cord said, "but also from Donna."

"Oh yes, Donna," Clint said. "I saw her for the first time in seven years today. What a shock."

"A shock?"

"Well, she was a darling little girl, but I didn't expect her to grow up and be so . . . so beautiful. I'm sure you've noticed."

Cord smiled and said, "Oh yeah, I've noticed."

Clint studied him. If Cord hadn't admitted to noticing, he would have thought the young man a liar. Now he wondered if Cord was as stuck on Donna as the sheriff seemed to be.

"Guess she must have a lot of young men riding out to see her," he said.

"Not that many."

"Oh? Why not? She hasn't got a regular fella, has she?"

"Her pa is kind of . . . protective."

"Oh, I see."

"He doesn't let too many fellas come out there."

"But he lets you."

"I work for him."

"You, uh, live out back in the bunkhouse, is that right?"

"That's right," Cord said. "Will you be staying at the place?"

"I don't know," Clint said. "I have a hotel room, and there doesn't seem to be room in the house."

"There's plenty of room in the bunkhouse," Cord said. "I'm the only one stayin' there—not that it's my place to invite you, but I wouldn't mind the company."

The young man was very good. He knew Clint was wondering about him and Donna Fox. Donna could very well have been in the bunkhouse with Cord the whole time her family was waiting for her. Clint wondered if Nelson ever thought about his daughter and his top hand.

"That's an idea I hadn't thought of," Clint said. "Maybe I'll talk to Nelson about it tomorrow at lunch. Will you be at lunch?"

"Me?" Cord asked, looking surprised. "Oh no. I'm hired help, Mr. Adams. I don't eat with the family."

"I see," Clint said. "Well, I'll probably see you out there over the next few days, so there's no use in you calling me Mr. Adams. The name's Clint."

"Well, much obliged, Clint," Cord said. "The name is Will."

"Will, do you come in here much?"

"Pretty often."

"They have a house-run poker game here?"

"No," Cord said, "just about everything but."

"Do they frown on private poker games?"

"Not that I know of, but I hardly ever see one in here, there's so much else to do."

"I can see that," Clint said. "Blackjack, faro, roulette, baccarat. Do you play?"

"A little bit of all of them, I guess."

"Let me ask you this, then." Clint lowered his voice. "Would you know which of these tables I should definitely stay away from?"

Cord turned and looked out at the room.

"I could probably give you a hint or two, Clint," he admitted, "though I wouldn't exactly call myself a gambling man."

"Well," Clint said, "even if you just . . . dabbled, I'm sure you'd know which table you had the least luck at."

"Clint," Cord said, "I've had bad luck at all of them, but let's see if I can't give you just a hint or two."

FIFTEEN

Will Cord was able to point out the dealers or croupiers who were particularly hard on the gamblers. Clint didn't play faro, and roulette was just too dependent on luck for his money. That left baccarat and blackjack. According to Cord, the Baccarat dealer was particularly good, or "lucky."

That left blackjack, and in the absence of poker, that was Clint's choice.

"Will you be playing tonight?" Clint asked Cord.

"Not on my salary," the young man said. "But if you don't mind, I'll watch."

"I don't mind."

There were two blackjack tables in the place, but there was only a seat at one of them. There were five seats at each table, and it was the fourth chair that was open at the second table. That suited Clint. He disliked sitting in any of the first three chairs, preferring what was generally known as "fourth street" or "fifth street."

He sat down in the fourth chair just in time to see the dealer build twenty-one on five cards, effectively beating everyone at the table.

"What's the buy-in?" he asked the dealer.

"Five-dollar minimum bet, friend," the dealer said. He was a black-haired man with bad bottom teeth and a weak jaw. It didn't take good teeth or a strong jaw to deal blackjack, though.

"And the maximum?"

"A hundred," the dealer said, "for now."

Clint took fifty dollars out of his pocket and bought ten five-dollar chips.

He bet one chip and the dealer promptly dealt himself blackjack, beating everyone on the table again.

Clint lost the next two hands, the dealer beating his eighteen with nineteen, and his nineteen with twenty. He decided to increase his bet on the basis of the odds. After losing three hands in a row, he figured he was due for a win. If the dealer beat him again by a point or two, he intended to quit.

He put twenty-five dollars on the line this time, and the dealer dealt him an ace of hearts and a king of diamonds.

Blackjack.

His $25 won him $62.50, as blackjack paid off two and half times his bet. He had $87.50 left on the table, and he let it ride.

The dealer dealt him a king and a jack for a total of twenty. After he had finished busting two of the other players and dealing the other two eighteen and nineteen, he turned over his own cards to reveal a seventeen. The dealer lost.

Clint doubled his money and now had $175 on the table, plus $10 left from his initial buy-in.

"Can we raise the limit?" he asked.

"You want to let the hundred and seventy-five ride?" the dealer asked.

"That's right."

"I'll need an okay," the dealer said.

"I'll wait," Clint said. He looked at the other players and asked, "Anyone mind waiting?"

"Mister," the man in the first seat said, "he's been beating our brains out all night. I, for one, will wait to see him taken."

The other players all nodded their agreement.

The blackjack dealer raised his hand and immediately a small man in a black suit appeared at his side.

"This gentleman wants to bet a hundred and seventy-five dollars."

The little man looked at Clint and asked, "If you hit this time, do you intend to let it ride?"

"I don't think so," Clint said. "If I win this hand I think I will have pushed it enough."

The little man looked at the dealer and said, "Go ahead, Len. Deal."

The other men got their bets down, all for ten or twenty dollars this time instead of five. They wanted to have money on the line if Clint beat the dealer.

The first man was dealt a fifteen. He took a

hit and busted, drawing an eight for twenty-three.

The second man caught a seventeen and stayed.

The man on Clint's right was dealt thirteen. He asked for a card and got a ten, busting.

Clint was dealt a twelve, and since the dealer's up card was a five he stood.

"You're standing on twelve?" asked the man on his right, who had taken a hit on thirteen.

"That's right."

The man on Clint's left, the fifth man, was dealt an eleven. He took another card, which turned out to be a ten, giving him twenty-one. If Clint had taken a card, the ten would have given him twenty-two and busted his hand.

"Good play," said the man to his right.

"That remains to be seen," Clint said, inclining his head toward the dealer.

The dealer had a five showing, and when he turned up his hole card it was a ten. With fifteen he had already beaten Clint, but he was bound by the house rules—"hit on sixteen, stand on seventeen"—to take another card. When he took it, it was a seven, giving him twenty two and busting his hand.

The table went wild, and so did the people watching the game, including Will Cord.

"Thank you," Clint said to the dealer and raked in his $350.

SIXTEEN

"All bets up, please," the dealer said. He glared at Clint when he put up a five-dollar chip, and then again when he busted Clint's hand and took the chip.

Clint played even for the next half hour, waiting for the time when he might take three hands in a row again. Once or twice he felt the time might be right and put up twenty-five dollars and lost, then he'd recoup the losses with five- and ten-dollar bets.

Finally the time came again and he decided to push it hard. He bet a hundred. The dealer glared at him and dealt out the cards. Clint bought a twenty—a jack and a queen—and beat the dealer's nineteen.

"I'd like to let it ride," he told the dealer, and everyone leaned into the table.

"One moment."

The dealer looked around, raised his hand, and the little man appeared again.

"He'd like to raise the limit again."

The little man eyed Clint, then looked at the chips on the table and saw that it was two hundred dollars. He looked at the dealer and nodded, then stood there to watch the hand being played.

The other players all doubled or tripled their bets to ride with Clint.

The dealer doled out the cards, and Clint bought a ten and a nine. The dealer was forced to stand when he revealed an eighteen.

Clint now had four hundred dollars on the table.

"What do you say?" he asked the little man in the dark suit.

"Give me a minute," the man said, and Clint knew that he didn't have the authority to okay the betting any further.

"Want a beer?" Will asked, leaning close to Clint.

"No," Clint said, "not while I'm playing cards."

"Are you really gonna let four hundred dollars ride?" he asked.

"Yep."

"Why? You already won what—three hundred or more?"

"More."

"Then why?"

Clint turned and looked at Will.

"You really don't gamble that much, do you?"

"No, why?"

"Because most of the time," Clint explained, "unless you're doing it for a living, it's not the money you do it for, it's the play."

"Not the money?"

"No."

Will shook his head.

"Look," Clint said, "what do I stand to lose on this hand?"

"Four hundred dollars."

"Wrong."

Will frowned and counted the chips again in his head.

"Looks like four hundred dollars to me."

"Oh, there's four hundred dollars there, all right," Clint said, "but it's not mine, it's theirs. See, I've still got my original fifty dollars in front of me."

Will nodded and said, "I think I understand." Then he frowned and shook his head and said, "No, I don't."

"I'll try to explain it to you later."

Word had gotten around that there was a big bet on the table and now there was a pack of people crowded around to watch. Clint was sort of surprised that four hundred dollars qualified as a big bet. He'd been in places before where thousands of dollars had to be put on the table before special permission was needed to raise a limit.

Before long the little man in the dark suit returned with a bigger man in a dark suit, but there the similarity ended. The taller man was obviously in command.

"This is the gentleman who would like to raise the limit," the little man said.

"My name is Bruce Stilwell," the larger man said. His dark hair was beginning to go gray, as was his mustache. "I manage this place."

"Clint Adams," he said. "Are you the man who can authorize this bet?"

"That's me," Stilwell said. He looked at the chips on the table. "That's a big bet."

"Oh, come now," Clint said, "you've seen bigger bets than that."

"Yes, I have," Stilwell said, "but not here."

"Look," Clint said, reaching for his chips, "if it's a problem I'll just take my money and go to bed."

"Uh, that won't be necessary," Stilwell said, putting his hand out. He looked at the dealer and said, "You can deal the cards." He looked at the other players and said, "Only Mr. Adams, please."

"Oh, no," Clint said.

"I beg your pardon?" Stilwell said.

"They're in the game too."

"Mr. Adams, this is a lot of money—"

"And you're trying to change the cards by eliminating the other players. If they don't play, I don't. I'll take my winnings—"

He reached for the chips and once again Stilwell put his arm out and said, "All right, Mr. Adams, have it your way." He looked at the dealer. "Deal to everyone."

"Yes, sir," the man said.

Stilwell, the little man in the dark suit, and all the other people leaned forward to watch the deal.

The first man got thirteen and stood with the dealer showing a six. The second man got fifteen, hit, and busted. The third man got eighteen and stood. The dealer dealt Clint an ace of spades and a queen of hearts.

Blackjack, his second one of the night, this one worth a thousand dollars.

Clint turned his head, looked at Will Cord, and said, "Kind of ruined the suspense, didn't it?"

SEVENTEEN

Clint left the blackjack table after that bet, a little more than a thousand ahead.

"Can I buy you a drink?" Stilwell asked.

"Sure," Clint said, then indicated Will Cord and added, "if you include my friend, here."

"Of course. I have a table in the back."

Clint and Will followed Bruce Stilwell to the back of the saloon, where he had a private table. Stilwell waved an arm and a blond saloon girl appeared.

"Beer?" Stilwell asked them.

"Sure," Clint said. Will nodded.

"Three beers, Sally."

"Right, boss."

As the girl left, Stilwell sat with his back to the wall. Since it was the man's private table Clint didn't feel he could ask him to move. Besides, there was a chair on the man's left that was just as good. Clint sat in it and slanted it so that no one could get behind him and he could see the entire room.

"I see you're a careful man," Stilwell said.

Clint didn't reply. Stilwell knew who he was, and why he had to be careful.

"Is blackjack your game, Mr. Adams?" Stilwell asked.

"No, not really."

"What is?"

"Poker."

Stilwell shook his head.

"Not much profit for the house in poker. Too many players."

"I understand that," Clint said. "I don't play in house games, anyway."

"Will you be in town long?"

"For a while."

"Really? Would you be interested in a private game sometime?"

"Sure, why not?" Clint said. "Looking to get your money back?"

"One way or another," Stilwell admitted, spreading his hands. "If not at blackjack, then why not poker?"

"Why not?" Clint said.

Sally returned with their beers and set them on the table.

"Thanks, honey," Stilwell said.

"Sure, boss."

Clint noticed Sally toss a glance Cord's way, but the young man didn't seem to notice.

"Saw you talking with the sheriff earlier," Stilwell said. "Is he giving you some trouble?"

"Not much."

"Because if he is, I could talk to him."

"You could?"

Stilwell nodded.

"I have some influence in town."

"I see," Clint said. "Well, as far as I'm concerned, Mr. Stilwell, he was just doing his job. I don't think I need you to . . . get involved."

"Well, if you change your mind you let me know, huh?" Stilwell said.

"Sure," Clint said. "I'm obliged for the offer—and for the beer."

"Yeah," Cord said, picking his mug up, "thanks."

"I don't think we've met," Stilwell said.

"Oh, I'm sorry," Clint said. "This is Will Cord, top hand for Nelson Fox."

"Ah, you work for Mr. Fox," Stilwell said, making no attempt to shake hands.

"That's right."

"Fine man."

"Yes, he is."

After that it was as if Cord ceased to exist. Stilwell spent the rest of the time talking to Clint and virtually ignoring the younger man. Clint did not appreciate that. He thought Cord should have been afforded the same consideration that he was—although it was true that Cord had not just taken the man for a thousand dollars.

Clint and Cord finished their beers, and then Clint slid his chair back.

"Leaving?" Stilwell asked.

Clint smiled and said, "I think I've had enough excitement for one night. Again, thanks for the beer."

"Anytime," Stilwell said, also standing. He extended his hand and added, "Thanks for the game."

"You're a good loser," Clint said.

"I'm also a good winner," Stilwell said. "Both are part of the game."

"I agree."

"See you tomorrow, I hope," Stilwell said. "I should have more information about a private game by then."

"I'll look forward to it," Clint said.

He and Cord walked away from the table.

"Where are you headed?" Clint asked.

"Back to the ranch, I guess."

"I'm goin' to bed," Clint said. "I guess I'll see you out there tomorrow."

"You, uh, want me to walk you back to your hotel, seeing as you're carrying all that money?"

"No, Will," Clint said, "I think I can handle it. Thanks."

When they stepped outside Will asked, "Are you really gonna play poker with him?"

"Why not?"

"Well . . . ain't he a professional gambler?"

"I suppose he is."

"Can you play with a professional?"

"Why not?" Clint asked, patting his pocket. "After all, I'll be using his money, won't I?"

EIGHTEEN

Clint woke early the next morning and had a light breakfast. Outside the streets were just as muddy as ever, but he was still unsure about staying out at the Fox place. There was too much going on, and most of it things he didn't know about. Still, staying in the bunkhouse didn't sound like such a bad idea. Maybe he'd see what the mood out at the ranch was today and make up his mind then.

He spent the morning sitting in a chair in front of the hotel, nodding at people as they went by and stared at him curiously. Obviously, everyone in town knew who he was now, and that might just be the deciding factor for him to stay out at the ranch.

Sheriff Grady came by at one point and stopped to talk.

"Heard you took Bruce Stilwell for a lot of money last night."

"I won some money, yes," Clint said, "but from the saloon, not from him."

"Same thing."

"He told me he manages the place."

"He does," the sheriff said, "but he also owns it."

"I see. How did you hear about the game?"

"It's right here." Grady handed him the local newspaper.

Clint unfolded the paper and looked at the front page.

"Gunsmith wins a thousand dollars from Cactus Hall," he read aloud.

"It's a big story hereabouts," Grady said. "And given your reputation, some other papers will probably pick it up as well."

"Jesus," Clint said under his breath. He handed the paper back.

"You must be used to this kind of thing by now," Grady said. "A man with a reputation like yours."

"Yeah," Clint said, "sure."

"Well," Grady said, "I gave Hiram—that's the editor of the paper—what for."

"Why?"

"For running this story without checking with me first," the lawman said. "You know what this is gonna do, don't you?"

"Sure," Clint said. "Some sodbuster who thinks he's good with a gun is going to show up here looking for me."

"That's right, and it's gonna be my job to get rid of him, not yours. Do you understand that?"

"Sure, Sheriff," Clint said, "I understand."

"I'd ask you to move on, but I understand you're visiting with your friends," Grady said. "Maybe it would be a good idea for you to go out and stay with them, instead of in town."

"Now that would bring the trouble out to them, wouldn't it?"

"Maybe," Grady said, "and maybe I can convince the trouble that you've moved on."

"That means I'd have to hide out there," Clint said. "That idea doesn't appeal to me much either, Sheriff."

"I guess hiding isn't the way you do things."

"Look, Sheriff," Clint said, "I don't go looking for trouble. But I don't run from it either. If word ever got around that I did that, I'd attract even more of it. Surely you can see that."

"Yeah," Grady said, folding the newspaper up and sticking it in his back pocket, "yeah, I guess I can see your point."

"Thanks."

"What are your plans for today?"

"Today I'm going back out to the Fox place to have lunch," Clint said. "While I'm there, I'll talk about where I'm going to stay."

"Well, I hope you understand when I say I ain't lookin' forward to havin' you here in town, Adams."

"Sure, Sheriff," Clint said, "I understand."

"Just doin' my job."

"Right."

NINETEEN

At lunch that day Clint approached Nelson
Fox with the idea of staying in the bunkhouse
with Will Cord.

"Sounds good to me," Nelson said.

"Me too!" Jeff said enthusiastically. He
wanted Clint around to talk to.

The idea also sat well with Carol. The only
one it didn't seem to appeal to was Donna,
although she tried to hide her displeasure.
Clint felt almost certain that this proved she
was seeing Will Cord. He wondered why her
mother and father couldn't see it as well.

"I'll pick up my gear later today," Clint said.

"I'll let Will know you're coming."

"That's okay," Clint said. "We met last night,
and it was actually his idea."

The words were out of his mouth before he
could stop them, and when he saw the momen-
tary frown on Donna's face he was sorry he'd
said them.

Will Cord was in for an earful.

• • •

Clint moved his gear in later that day, and over the next three days he stayed out of town and around the Fox place. He did some hunting with Nelson Fox, and some with Jeff, but never with Nelson and Jeff at the same time. Other times, when he went with Jeff, Will Cord came along. Will and Jeff seemed to have a fairly cordial attitude toward one another, while Jeff and his father rarely seemed to converse unless they had to.

He watched Will and Donna carefully and the coolness he saw caused him to believe that he had been right about them. They had obviously been meeting in the bunkhouse, which they could not do now because Clint was staying there.

On the fourth day Clint found himself out hunting for varmints with Cord, while Nelson and Jeff were tending to their everyday chores. Carol said she was having trouble with varmints getting into their supplies, and Clint offered to go out with Cord to hunt for them.

"I'm sorry about Donna," Clint said.

Cord hesitated, then asked, "What about her?"

"She's obviously upset with you for suggesting I stay in the bunkhouse."

Cord looked at Clint quickly before he could stop himself.

"Yeah, I let it slip that it was your idea," Clint said. "Sorry."

Cord hesitated again, then asked, "How

could you tell what was going on between us when her own parents can't see it?"

"They're too close to it," Clint said. "Besides, they have other problems."

"I know."

"You do?"

Cord nodded.

"What's the problem with Jeff?"

"Is there a problem with Jeff?" Cord asked.

"I thought you said you knew about it."

"I know about their business problems," Cord said, "not their personal problems."

"But, if you and Donna are ... I mean, wouldn't you know about their personal problems from her?"

"Only if she knows about them, which I guess she doesn't."

"Good point."

They walked along a little further, their rifles ready in their hands.

"What kind of business problems are they having?" Clint asked suddenly.

"I really shouldn't talk about it, but since you're a friend of theirs ... Business just isn't good. That's why I'm the only full-time hand."

"What's the problem?"

"Competition."

"Oh, I heard something about someone named McFall."

"That's him," Cord said, "Patrick McFall. He came into the territory about a year back and brought a lot of money with him. He's got a bigger operation than Mr. Fox, and he's able to get better horses, break them quicker, and have them ready for sale quicker."

"Nelson's never been afraid of competition."

"He's not afraid," Cord said, "but there's a little bit more going on than just competition. It's turned into a downright feud."

"Why a feud?"

"They don't like each other," Cord said, "and McFall's got a son who has his eye on Donna."

"I see. How big a family does McFall have?"

"He's got two sons and a daughter. One son is about twenty-four, and the other one is almost thirty. He's the ramrod of the outfit, name of Red McFall."

"What's Red like?" Clint asked.

"Trouble," Cord said.

"Figures," Clint said.

"There goes a critter!" Cord cried.

Both men raised their rifles and fired, and the animal leapt into the air and then fell to the ground dead.

"Mine," Cord said.

"I don't think so."

"Want to bet?"

"How much?"

Cord hesitated, then said, "Five dollars?"

Clint smiled and said, "You're on."

TWENTY

Stephen Robinson couldn't believe his luck.

He was sitting in a saloon in Camden, Minnesota, reading a newspaper, and there it was, right in front of his eyes. A story about Clint Adams cleaning out a saloon blackjack game in North Bend, a town in the Dakotas just south of the Canadian border.

Robinson had come down from the Lake of the Woods and entered the United States at Minnesota. If he'd taken a slightly different route, one more to the west, he would have entered in the Dakotas.

Still, he now knew where the Gunsmith was, and with a little luck and some hard riding he'd get to North Bend before the man left.

It was time for him to leave Minnesota, anyway. He'd killed his first American in a gunfight there, in a town called Sentinel, and then his second yesterday here in Camden. Both were fair fights and the law couldn't touch him, but word traveled fast about the man who wore the gun with a silver handle.

The silver on the butt of his gun was an idea he got just before he left Canada, and he was convinced it was a good one. It added some flash to the reputation he was building, a reputation that would become legendary when he reached the Dakotas, where the Gunsmith was waiting to make the Canadian Gun the most famous gunman in history.

TWENTY-ONE

The evening of Clint's fourth day in North Bend, Nelson and Carol Fox told him that Brenda Tyler was coming to dinner that night.

"That's nice," he said.

"That's all you have to say?" Carol asked, teasing him. "You liked her a lot that first day. I can't understand why you haven't seen her again."

Clint had explained to Nelson the problem he had with staying in town, and they hadn't mentioned this to Carol. She was so satisfied with him staying at their place that she'd never asked any questions.

Clint didn't want to worry her by telling her that he was staying out of town to avoid trouble. Actually, he'd been thinking lately of going back into town, both to see Brenda Tyler and to see about that poker game with Bruce Stilwell.

"I just haven't had the time," Clint said.

"What have you been doing?"

"I've been hunting critters for you."

"Oh you . . ." she said.

Later, on the porch, Nelson said, "You're thinkin' about goin' into town, aren't you?"

"Yes."

"What for?"

"I can't hide out here, Nelson," Clint explained. "I told that to the sheriff already."

"Stayin' out of trouble is not the same as hidin'," Nelson said.

"There's not that much of a difference."

"All right," Nelson said, "if you want to go to town, I'll go with you."

"No," Clint said, "that's not a good idea."

"Why not?"

"Look," Clint said, "I don't need an escort—"

"You need somebody to watch your back."

"I'll ask Will if he wants to go to town," Clint said. "How's that?"

"Well, he is a good shot."

"I know," Clint said, "I nearly lost five dollars to him."

"Nearly?"

"I'll tell you about it another time. Where does a man find a bath around here? There's a lady coming to dinner."

TWENTY-TWO

Clint's dilemma about going to town was solved when he asked Nelson how Brenda was getting out to his place.

"She'll probably ride out."

"Alone?"

Clint wouldn't have that so he rode into North Bend that evening and stopped in front of Brenda Tyler's store. Nelson had told him that she lived upstairs.

"Will she close early to come out here for dinner?" he'd asked.

"Brenda's a good businesswoman, Clint," Nelson had said. "She'll find someone to take care of the store while she comes to dinner. That store won't close one minute before it's supposed to."

Clint dismounted and entered the store, expecting to find Brenda behind the counter. When he walked in, a woman in her fifties with salt-and-pepper hair looked at him from behind the counter and smiled.

"May I help you?"

"Yes, I was looking for Brenda."

"Oh, she's not here right now."

"Is she upstairs changing for dinner?"

The woman's face registered surprise.

"Why yes, she is. How did you know that?"

"I'm here to escort her out to the Fox place."

"Why, how nice," the woman said. "I'll go and tell her. Uh, what's your name?"

"Clint Adams."

"Adams," the woman repeated, the name obviously familiar to her. Why not? It was familiar to anyone who had read that newspaper story.

"And your name?"

"Oh, well, my name is Dorrie Washburn," she said, and then added, "Mrs. Washburn . . . widowed."

"Well, thank you for your help, Mrs. Washburn," he said, "and I'm so sorry about your husband."

"It was . . . years ago."

"Well, I'm sure a charming woman like you won't stay unmarried much longer. You must have a long line of suitors."

"Well . . . not very long . . ." she said, turning shy on him.

"I'm sure you're just being modest."

"I'll, uh, just go up and, uh, tell Brenda you're here."

"Thank you."

Dorrie went through the curtained doorway behind the counter, and Clint walked to the front window to look outside. It was a clear, crisp day, and there didn't seem to be a hint of trouble in the air. He knew how deceiving that could be, though, like the calm before the storm.

Before long Dorrie was back.

"She'll be right down, Mr. Adams."

"Thank you."

"She was, uh, surprised that you were here."

"Well," Clint said, with a smile, "it was meant to be a surprise."

"Ah . . ." Dorrie said.

"Don't let me keep you from you work," Clint said.

"I, uh, don't really work here," Dorrie said. "I just help Brenda when she needs it."

"A good neighbor."

"Why, yes. . . ."

"She's very lucky to have a friend like you," Clint said. "I'm sure a woman of your maturity and experience is of help to her in many, many other ways as well."

"Oh, well . . . how kind of you to say so, Mr. Adams," the woman said, placing one hand against her breast and almost simpering.

"I'll just stand aside and you pretend I'm not even here," he said.

He placed his hands behind his back and took up a position over by the boots. Dorrie Washburn tried to do her work but found herself glancing over at him every few moments, at which time he'd give her as big a smile as he could muster.

About fifteen minutes later Brenda Tyler
appeared. She was wearing a powder-blue
shirt, black riding skirt, and black boots.
She was also wearing black leather riding
gloves. As she passed Dorrie Washburn, she
put her hand on the woman's shoulder and
smiled at her.

"Why, Clint," she said, turning the smile
on him and widening it, "I didn't expect an
escort."

"It's not safe for a young woman to ride
alone," he said.

"I've ridden out to the Fox house many
times," Brenda said. "There's never been any
danger."

"I didn't think there would be any harm in
my escorting you, Brenda," he said.

"Well, of course there's no harm," she said,
"I just didn't expect it. It's very kind of you."

"Is your horse at the livery?" he asked.

"Yes."

"Why don't I walk you over there, then?"
he said.

"Thank you . . . again." She turned and said
to Dorrie, "You can close and leave at six,
Dorrie, and thanks again for your help."

"Not at all, dear."

"Yes, Mrs. Washburn," Clint said, "thank
you for your help, and your company."

"You're very welcome, Mr. Adams. Have a
pleasant evening, you two."

Outside Brenda looked at Clint strangely
and asked, "How did you do that?"

"Do what?"

"Reduce Dorrie to . . . to a simpering young girl," she said. "She's absolutely charmed by you!"

"You don't need to sound so surprised," Clint said. "I am a fairly charming fellow, you know."

"No," Brenda said, "I don't know . . . and I have a feeling I should be very careful while you're showing me just how charming you are."

"Oh, I'd think that by now you'd have had lots of experience with charming men," he said.

"See," she said, pointing a finger at him, "there you go already. I have the feeling you're a very dangerous man, Clint Adams."

"Why Miss Tyler," Clint said, "I don't have any idea what you're talking about."

TWENTY-THREE

Rufus saddled Brenda's horse while she and Clint waited outside. When he walked her horse out, the filly looked like she could have been an offspring of Duke's, if he hadn't been gelded. She was smaller than he was but just as black.

"Huh," Rufus said, looking from the filly to Duke, "could be father and daughter."

Clint walked over to the filly and ran his hands over her lines.

"She's a beauty," Clint said to Brenda.

"Yes, she is," Brenda said. "Rufus takes good care of her for me."

"Some folks trust me with their animals," Rufus said, with an attitude. He still hadn't forgiven Clint for taking Duke out of his care.

"She's a beautiful animal," Clint said. "What is she, about three?"

"Almost," Brenda said.

"What's her name?"

Brenda made a face and said, "Princess. I know it's not very original but . . ."

"It fits her," Clint said, finishing her thought.

"Yes."

Duke was paying very little attention to the filly.

"Duke doesn't seem to like her," Brenda said,

"What does he know?" Clint said. "He's just a horse."

He helped her mount up, then climbed aboard Duke.

"You know where to find me, Miz Brenda, if you get back late," Rufus said.

"I know, Rufus," she said. "Thanks."

The liveryman gave Clint a hard look, then turned away and stalked into the stable.

They rode in tandem to the Fox place, Clint not allowing Duke to stretch out his legs for fear the filly wouldn't be able to keep up.

"We could go faster, you know," she said. "Or don't you think Princess can keep up with Duke?"

"No offense, Brenda," Clint said, "but I haven't found a horse yet that could keep up with Duke."

"Well, I don't mean to race him," Brenda said, "but you can go a little faster. Princess won't break."

"All right, then," Clint said, "a little faster."

When Clint reached the house he turned and watched as Brenda covered the last twenty yards and then stopped next to him. Both she and the filly were breathing hard.

"You're snotty," she said to him.

"Well, I'm sorry—"

"Don't apologize," she said, giving him a bold look. "I like snotty—in the right places."

He looked right back at her and said, "I'll remember that."

At that moment the door to the house opened and Nelson, Carol, and Donna came pouring out.

"About time you two got here," Nelson shouted. "Carol was starting to think you had run off with each other."

"I said no such thing," Carol said. "That was you, Nels."

"Well, no matter," Nelson said, "they're here now. Where's Jeff? I wanted him to take care of their horses. Oh, here he comes."

Jeff came running over from the direction of the corral while Clint dismounted and helped Brenda down. Brenda was immediately hugged by Carol and then Donna, and Clint got pushed off a little to the side.

"Here you go, Jeff," Clint said, handing him the reins of both horses.

"Wow," Jeff said, "they look like they could be father and daughter."

"So they do," Clint said.

"Well, what do you think of the little filly?" Nelson asked, patting the little black's neck.

"I like her just fine, Nels," Clint said, "and the horse isn't bad either."

TWENTY-FOUR

The McFall brothers, Red and Ben, rode into North Bend from the east just minutes after Clint and Brenda Tyler rode out to the west.

"Where you headin', little brother?" Red asked.

"The saloon, I guess."

"I'll meet you over there, then," Red said. "From there we'll go to the bank and take care of business for Pa."

"I guess I know where you're goin' first," Ben said, "stuck on that Brenda like you are."

"Oh yeah," Red said, "like you ain't stuck on that little Donna Fox, huh?"

Red reached out to pull his brother's hat down over his eyes, but Ben shied away successfully. The brothers laughed and rode off in their separate directions.

Red rode up to Brenda's store and dismounted, tying his horse to the hitching post out front. When he entered he saw the old woman, Dorrie Washburn, behind the counter instead of Brenda.

"Where's Brenda, Dorrie?" he demanded.

Dorrie looked up from her work and when she saw Red McFall her eyes narrowed. She had no use for the McFalls, not the sons and not their father. Johnny-come-latelies they were in North Bend, and she had no use for their kind.

"She's not here."

"Oh yeah?" Red asked. He didn't like Dorrie any more than she liked him. "Suppose I just go upstairs and have a look, huh?"

"You'll do nothing of the kind, young man," Dorrie snapped, eyes flashing.

Red approached the counter and leaned over it.

"You gonna stop me, old woman?"

"I am."

He sneered and said, "That's a good way to get yourself hurt."

Dorrie glared at Red McFall. For a handsome man—six two with flaming red hair and a firm jaw—he had a decidedly ugly personality. She had often thought he'd be perfect for Brenda if he were just a nicer man—like that Clint Adams. There was a man with a big reputation, but still just as nice as could be.

"You go ahead and hurt me, Red McFall," Dorrie said, "but if you do, you better kill me."

Red stared at the old woman for a few moments, then backed off, deciding that she was too crazy to kill.

"You're a tough old bird, Dorrie."

"Don't you be calling me by my first name,

Red McFall! I cringe when I hear you say it."

"Why don't I just fire a shot through the ceiling?" Red asked, drawing his gun. "Maybe that'll bring Brenda running down, huh?"

"I told you she ain't here."

"Don't give me that," he said. "She never leaves before closing."

"Not usually, but today she went out to the Fox place for dinner."

"The Fox place, huh?" Red said. "I don't know what she sees in those people. My pa is gonna grind Nelson Fox into the ground."

"Your pa ain't man enough to—"

Red McFall could take insults and slurs against himself, or even his brother, but not against his kid sister, and not against his father. Before Dorrie could finish, Red lashed out at her with his gun. The sight caught her on the cheek and tore it open. She screamed and clasped her hands to her bloody cheek.

"You animal!"

"Your own fault, old woman," Red said, holstering the gun. "You shouldn't ought to talk against my pa."

"You wait, Red McFall," Dorrie said, "you'll get yours."

"Did Brenda ride out alone?"

Blood seeped between Dorrie's fingers as she got an idea.

"No, she didn't," she said to Red. "She rode off with a man."

"A man? What man?"

"A good and decent man, Red McFall. She rode off with Clint Adams."

"Clint Adams?"

"Yes, you know him," she said. "The Gun-smith. Why don't you ride after them? They just left. Ride after them and see if you can stand up to a man like Clint Adams. Ride after them so he can shoot you down like the animal you are."

Red was tempted to strike Dorrie again, but he decided not to. There was going to be hell to pay with his pa for hitting her once already.

"Don't think I'm afraid of the likes of Clint Adams, old woman," Red said. "I could stand against him any day."

"Sure you could," she said, "with you pa and your brother maybe, but not alone."

"I should tear your face open on the other side, old lady," he said, "but you ain't worth the effort."

Red turned and left the store, and Dorrie Washburn started to cry. She'd be damned if she'd cry in front of him, no matter how much her cheek hurt. Now that he was gone, though, the tears flowed hotly. She looked around for a cloth to hold to her cheek and then she left the store to go to the doctor's.

When Ben McFall saw his brother walk into the saloon, he knew something was wrong. He could always tell when his broth-er was angry. His face got almost as red as his hair.

"What's wrong, Red?"

"Dorrie Washburn says Brenda rode off with Clint Adams to the Fox ranch."

"Adams?" Ben said, swallowing. "Ain't he the one who won all that money from Bruce Stilwell? Ain't he the one they call the Gunsmith?"

"So what? You don't think I'm afraid of him, do you?" Red demanded.

"N-no, Red, I don't think that at all."

"Damned right I ain't. Come on."

"Where we goin'? To the bank?"

"To hell with the bank," Red said. "We're going back to the ranch."

"What for?" Ben asked. "We got business to do for Pa. He's gonna be real mad—"

"He ain't gonna be mad, Ben," Red said. "This is his business too. He's got to know that Nelson Fox has hired the Gunsmith."

"Hired him?"

"That's right," Red McFall said. "Nelson Fox has gone and hired himself a gunman. He just upped the ante in this game."

TWENTY-FIVE

Dinner that night was slightly embarrassing. Well, actually, it was very embarrassing. Nelson and Carol were doing their damnedest to match Clint and Brenda up, while they both squirmed uncomfortably. The funny thing to Clint was that when he and Brenda found themselves on the front porch alone, she apologized to him.

"I was going to apologize to you," Clint said.

"Well, actually," she said, "I don't think we need to apologize for anything. Nelson and Carol are just being . . ."

"Nosy? Pushy? Pains in the ass?"

"Yes," Brenda said, "I couldn't have put it better, nosy, pushy pains in the ass."

"They mean well."

"It's always the people who mean well who are the most embarrassing."

"Have they done this to you before?"

"They've tried to fix me up once or twice before," she replied, "but never quite with this much . . . vigor."

"You know what we should do?" Clint asked.

"What?"

"We should saddle our horses and get the hell out of here."

Brenda laughed and said, "Wouldn't that be rude?"

"Yes," he said, "it would."

She laughed again and said, "Let's do it."

Together they bounded off the porch and ran for the barn.

Red and Ben McFall rode hell-for-leather back to their ranch to give their father the news.

"Where did you hear this from?" Patrick McFall asked after he'd listened to the story.

"That old biddy Dorrie Washburn."

"Dorrie is good friends with Brenda," McFall said. "She'd know what she was talking about."

"Oh, she knew all right," Red said. "She wouldn't have lied to me, Pa."

Patrick McFall was a big man, six three, in his mid-fifties, with black eyebrows but white hair. He was an imposing presence who ruled his family with an iron hand. Even now Ben was getting nervous because of the look on his father's face.

"Did you hurt her, Red?"

"Well, Pa—"

"Did you?"

"Well . . . yeah, I did, but not real bad—I mean, her face will heal—"

Patrick McFall knew damn well how his oldest son liked to use his gun. He closed the gap between himself and Red and stood nose to nose with him.

"You struck a woman, boy?"

"I didn't mean to, Pa—"

"How do you not mean to hit a woman and end up doing it?"

"Well, she said some things—"

"What could she have said that would make you do something like that?"

"She said bad things about you."

That stopped Patrick McFall.

"About me?"

"Yeah, Pa."

"You were standing up for me?"

"That's right, Pa," Red said, seizing on that, "I was standin' up for you."

McFall stared at his son for a few moments and just when Red relaxed, thinking he was out of the woods, Patrick McFall's massive hand came around and crashed into the side of his head. The blow made his cheek sting and his ear ring, and for a moment, out of instinct, he lifted his hand as if to strike back.

"You want to try me, boy?" the elder McFall asked tightly.

They stood that way for a few moments. Five feet away Ben could feel the tension, and it was making his heart pound. He would never have raised a hand against his father, no matter what. He was only five ten and whipcord thin, and the old man would have whipped his butt for sure. However, he wouldn't have minded seeing the old man and Red go at it. Red was nearly as big, not as heavy, but younger.

"No, Pa," Red said finally, "I ain't gonna try you."

Patrick brought his hand around again and both Ben and Red flinched. However, instead of striking Red again he put his hand on the back of the younger man's neck.

"It's good that you stick up for your pa, boy," the old man said. "It makes me proud."

"Uh, thanks, Pa."

"But you can't go around hitting old women, son," the man continued. "I'm gonna have to do some heavy talkin' with the sheriff when he comes out here."

"I'm sorry, Pa," Red said, "it won't happen again."

"I know it won't, boy." Patrick took his hand away from the back of his oldest son's neck and tapped him on the cheek with the palm of his hand. "I know it won't."

"Pa?" Ben asked. "What are we gonna do about Nelson Fox hiring a gunman?"

Patrick looked at his youngest son and said, "Why, we'll do what's fair, son."

Ben frowned and asked, "What's that?"

Patrick smiled. He always had the answer for whatever trouble arose.

"We'll hire a gunman of our own."

TWENTY-SIX

On the way back to town Clint and Brenda stopped off at a spot she said she liked very much, by a running brook. It was too shallow to have any fish, shallow enough to walk in. She said she enjoyed just coming out sometimes and sitting by it.

"And thinking," she said.

"About what?"

They had dismounted, and both animals were drinking from the water. Clint and Brenda were sitting side by side gazing out over the brook.

"Oh, just about what might have been."

"Lots of people think about that."

"Do they?"

"Sure."

"And you've known lots of people, haven't you?"

"My fair share," he said, then added, "or a few more."

"You travel quite a bit, don't you?"

"Yes."

"Is that because of . . . your reputation?" she asked. "If I'm being too nosy, please let me know."

"You're not."

"Is it difficult for you to settle down in one place because of . . . of who you are?"

"It might be," he said, "but that's not why I travel so much."

"Then why?"

"Simply because I like it."

"What kinds of places have you been to?"

"Oh, San Francisco, Denver, St. Louis, New Orleans, Kentucky, New York—"

"And other countries?"

He nodded.

"Those too," he said. "South America, England, Australia—"

"Australia?"

"Do you know it?"

"I've read about it," she said. "That's a long way away."

"Yes, it is."

She shook her head and said, "I wish I could travel."

"Why don't you?"

"I can't afford to," she said. "I have to keep the shop running."

"Why not sell it and use the money to travel?" he asked.

"Oh, I couldn't do that," she said.

"Why not?"

"My father started the shop years ago, and when he died last year I swore to him on his deathbed that I'd keep it going for him."

"He's dead, Brenda," Clint said. "He can't hold you to that."

"I know," she said, "but I can."

"Brenda—"

"I should get back now," she said, standing up. "You don't have to take me back, you know."

"Yes, I know," he said, "but I want to."

"All right," she said, smiling.

After Red McFall gave his father the news, he decided to ride back to town.

"Why?" Ben asked while his brother saddled his horse.

"We didn't finish Pa's business," Red said.

"That the real reason?" Ben asked.

"You don't have to come, you know," Red said. "I can handle it."

Ben frowned.

"Handle what?"

"Pa's business."

"I don't think you should go back to town so soon, Red."

"So soon after what?"

"After what you did to that woman," Ben said. "Pa wants to talk to the sheriff—"

"Ah, it's her word against mine," Red said. "Nobody saw me."

Ben regarded his brother critically for a moment, then said, "You want to go back to see Brenda, don't you?"

Finished saddling his mount, Red turned and said to Ben, "Mind your own business, little brother."

"I'm just trying to keep you out of trouble, Red," Ben said.

"Remember something, Ben."

"What?"

"You're the little brother," Red explained, "and I'm the big brother. I'm the one who's supposed to keep you out of trouble. Okay?"

"Okay, Red."

Red turned his horse around, mounted up, and looked down at his brother.

"I'll see you later."

"Sure, Red."

Ben watched as his brother rode away, thinking, big brother or not, Red was riding into trouble.

TWENTY-SEVEN

Clint and Brenda rode up to the livery and Rufus came out, as if he had been waiting for them.

"Yours?" he asked Clint.

"Just for a little while," Clint said. "I'll be leaving later."

"Figures."

He took the reins of both horses and led them into the stable.

"Do you think he'll ever forgive you?" Brenda asked.

"I don't know," Clint said. "You know him better than I do." Then he thought, who cares?

"I don't think anyone knows Rufus very well," she said. "He came here a year ago and bought the stable. I don't think he—"

"Why are we talking about Rufus?" Clint asked, interrupting her.

"You started it."

"I know."

They walked along the street until they reached Brenda's store, which was locked up tight.

"Looks like Mrs. Washburn did her job," Clint said.

Brenda unlocked the door with her key and opened it. It was dark inside.

"Well . . . good night," she said, turning to face him.

"You should let me come inside with you," he said. "It's dark."

"I'll be all right."

"I insist."

She studied him for a moment, her look speculative, and then she said, "Well, all right."

"I'll go first."

He went inside and she came in behind him.

"There's a lamp to the right," she said. "On the wall."

He reached for the wall, found it, and realized it was not a gaslit lamp. He produced a match from his pocket, struck it to life, and lit the lamp. Immediately the place was bathed in light.

Behind him he heard Brenda close the door.

"It looks all right," she said.

"I'd better look in the back," he said to her, "just to be safe."

"All right."

He crossed the room and went behind the counter and through the curtained doorway. He found himself in a hallway. To his right was a stairway, no doubt leading to her apartment. On the left was an open doorway. He struck another match and by its glow saw that this led to a storeroom.

He went back through the curtain and found her standing on the other side of the counter, staring down at it with a curious look on her face.

"What's wrong?"

"This," she said, pointing.

He saw what she was pointing at. There were a few dried, dark drops on the countertop.

"It looks like blood," he said.

"That's what I thought," she said, looking around with an agitated expression on her face. "What happened here?"

"Don't panic," he said. "The place looks fine. There's nothing out of place, is there?"

"No," she said, but her tone was unsure.

"It looks fine to me."

He touched the drops and then scraped them with a fingernail. They came off and wedged beneath his nail. He used another nail to pry them out.

"Blood?" she asked.

"Yes."

"Something happened here," she said, whipping her head back and forth, looking around anxiously. "Something may have happened to Dorrie."

"I guess so," Clint said. "But if something did, there's no other indication."

"How do we find out, then?"

"Simple," he said. "We ask the sheriff, or Dorrie."

She turned and looked at him.

"Will you go with me, Clint?"

"Are you sure you don't want to wait until morning?" he asked. "Or let me go and check on it?"

"No," she said, shaking her head. "This is my place. If something happened here, I want to find out about it now."

"Well," he asked, "who do you want to ask first?"

Across the street Red McFall stood in a doorway, watching the front door of Brenda Tyler's store. After Adams and Brenda went inside, he held his breath, waiting for the lamp to be lit upstairs. Instead, however, the lamp had been lit downstairs.

After a while he wondered what they were doing downstairs for so long. He was about to cross the street and see what he could see through the window when suddenly the lamp went out and the door opened. Both Adams and Brenda came out, Brenda closing the door behind her. They started off down the street. He watched them for half a block, then stepped out and followed them.

TWENTY-EIGHT

When Clint and Brenda entered the sheriff's office, Jack Grady hastily stood up behind his desk.

"Brenda," he said, and then as an afterthought, "Adams."

"Jack," Brenda said, "something happened at my store while I was away tonight. Do you know anything about it?"

"Yeah, I do, Brenda," Grady said. "Why don't you sit down—"

"What happened, Jack?" Brenda asked impatiently, "what happened to Dorrie?"

"She's all right, Brenda," Grady said. "Doc came to get me as soon as he finished patching her up—"

"Patching her up?" Brenda shouted. "I thought you just told me she was all right!"

"She is—"

"Then why did Doc have to patch her up?"

"Well, she did have a little accident."

"Little, Jack?"

"Well . . . her face got cut pretty bad."

"From what?"

"Well . . ." The sheriff looked decidedly uncomfortable, but Clint made the decision to let Brenda go right on handling the situation. She was doing fine.

"Jack?"

"She got cut by . . . by a gun sight."

"A gun? Who cut her with a gun?"

"A gun sight, Brenda," Grady said. "The part on the front of the barrel that—"

"I know what a damned gun sight is, Jack!" Brenda snapped. "Why are you beating around the bush? Get to it!"

Grady took a deep breath, tossed a helpless look at Clint, and then spoke.

"She says Red McFall hit her with his gun."

"Red McFall?" Brenda said. "That animal! Why would he hurt Dorrie?"

"She says he wanted to know where you were."

"And she wouldn't tell him?"

"That's what she says."

"Why do you keep saying 'she says,' Jack?" Brenda demanded. "Did Red hit her, or didn't he?"

"Well, she says—"

"You haven't talked to him, have you?"

"Well . . . no . . ."

"Because you're afraid of him!"

"Brenda," Grady said, "you got to understand—"

"And you're afraid of his father, the mighty Patrick McFall, right?"

"Brenda—"

"Well, are you or are you not going to arrest Red McFall for assault?"

"I can't, Brenda—"

"Why not?"

"There weren't any witnesses—"

"No witnesses? How about Dorrie? Isn't she witness enough?"

"She's the victim, Brenda," Grady said. "I need a witness to the assault—"

"That's nonsense, Jack Grady, and you know it!" she snapped. "I'm truly disappointed in you. I would never have imagined that you'd let a man get away with striking a woman. You're not only a poor excuse for a Sheriff, Jack, but a poor excuse for a man."

"Brenda—"

She ignored Grady and turned to Clint.

"I have to go and see Dorrie," she said. "She got hurt because of me."

"Bren—" Grady said.

"I don't want to hear any more from you, Jack," she said. "In fact, I don't want to talk to you again . . . ever!" She turned back to Clint and asked, "Will you come with me?"

"Sure."

She glared at Grady one more time, who looked to Clint for some sort of support or sympathy and got neither.

"Adams—"

If it was true that this Red McFall had struck the woman and Grady was letting him get away with it, then Clint agreed with everything Brenda had said.

"Can't help you, Sheriff," Clint said, and followed Brenda out.

Red McFall stood across the street from the sheriff's office, waiting for Clint and Brenda to come out. It wasn't hard to figure out what they were doing there. Brenda had figured out that something had happened in her store, and by now the sheriff had told her what. Up until now, though, the sheriff had made no move to do anything about it, which meant he was smart. McFall knew, however, that Grady was soft, and maybe a strong woman like Brenda would be able to force him into something.

For Grady's sake, Red McFall hoped that wasn't the case. Just to be on the safe side, however, he decided to do something about it right now.

He was crossing the street to the sheriff's office when the door opened and Clint and Brenda stepped out.

TWENTY-NINE

"It's him," Brenda said.

"Who?" Clint asked.

"Red McFall," she said, "coming across the street toward us."

Clint saw a tall, red-haired man crossing the street, walking purposefully toward them.

"We haven't talked to Dorrie yet, Brenda," he said. "We don't know the whole story."

"I don't need to know the whole story, Clint," she said. "I know Red McFall."

"How well?"

She looked at him and said, "Not as well as he would like."

"Brenda!" Red McFall called out.

"I see you coming, Red," Brenda replied. "I'm not going anywhere."

"Where did you go this evening?" McFall demanded, joining them on the boardwalk. "With him?"

114

"As a matter of fact," Brenda said, "I was with Clint, but where I was is none of your business."

"It damned sure is my business," McFall said. He looked at Clint and asked, "What are you doing with my fiancée?"

"I am not your fiancée," Brenda snapped. "Stop telling people that, Red. I wouldn't marry you if my life depended on it."

"Mister," McFall said to Clint, "as you can see, we're about to have us a lovers' spat, so I'd suggest you just move on."

Before Clint could say anything Brenda demanded, "What did you do to Dorrie?"

"Your friend Dorrie should learn better manners," McFall said.

"You hit her, didn't you?"

For a moment Clint thought the man was going to deny it, but then he said, "She had it comin'."

"You're an animal, Red," Brenda said, and then for good measure she slapped him across the face.

She hit him hard enough to shock him and rock his head back. Clint saw the crazed look in the man's eyes and knew he was going to try to hit her back. Red swung his right hand, saying, "Bitch!" but Clint stepped between them and blocked the blow with his elbow. He then hit McFall right on the point of the jaw, knocking the man into the street and on his back.

"Yeah!" Brenda shouted. "That's where you belong, Red, in the street!"

McFall lay on his back in the street for a few seconds, trying to clear his head, and Clint hoped that he wasn't going to do something rash.

"Clint," Brenda warned, "watch him. He's crazy."

Clint watched, and Red McFall did do something rash. He went for his gun.

Clint pushed Brenda away from him with his left hand just in case McFall got off a stray shot. With his right hand, though, he drew his gun and shot Red McFall in the left hip with no problem. The force of the bullet stunned McFall and his gun fell from his hand.

"What the hell—" Sheriff Grady shouted as he came out of his office. He stopped short, looked at Clint, and then looked at Red McFall, who was clutching his hip and rocking back and forth.

"Oh, Jesus, Adams," Grady said, "now you've gone and done it."

"He drew first, Sheriff," Clint said.

Grady looked at McFall, then at Brenda, then at Clint, and then back at the injured McFall.

THIRTY

It took some time for the sheriff to get McFall over to the doctor and have him looked at and then send someone out to the McFall ranch to tell Red's father what had happened. In the meantime, Clint and Brenda went over to see how Dorrie was doing.

"Be back in my office, Adams," Grady warned as Clint and Brenda walked away. "Back in my office in half an hour."

Clint nodded and walked off with Brenda.

"There's going to be trouble now, Clint," Brenda said. "It's my fault."

"It's not your fault, Brenda."

"Yes, it is," she said. "If I hadn't egged Red on, if I hadn't hit him he wouldn't have tried to hit me, and then you wouldn't have shot him."

"A man like Red McFall," Clint said, "is going to get himself shot sooner or later."

"That may be," she said, "but now you're going to have to deal with his father, Pat McFall."

"I'll handle that when the time comes, Brenda," Clint said. "Right now let's go and see how your friend is."

Dorrie assured Brenda that she would be fine, but Brenda insisted on staying and making her something to eat.

"I have to watch out for her, Clint," she said, hoping he'd understand.

"It's all right, Brenda," Clint said at the front door of Dorrie's house. "I understand. I have to go and talk to the sheriff, anyway."

"Do you think Red will die, Clint?"

"Not from a bullet in the hip he won't," Clint said.

"Let me know what happens, all right?" she asked. "I mean with you and—"

"Don't worry, Brenda," Clint said, cutting her off, "just take care of your friend."

"But you will let me know what happens?"

"Yes, I will."

"Promise?"

"I promise."

Impulsively she stood on her toes and kissed his mouth, a soft, fleeting touch of her full mouth that he took as a promise of things to come.

He left the house and headed for the sheriff's office.

THIRTY-ONE

When Clint walked into the sheriff's office for the second time that night, the man rose once again, this time very agitated.

"I just came from the doctor's office," Grady said.

"So?"

"He says your bullet might keep Red McFall from ever walkin' normal again. He says Red might walk with a limp for the rest of his life."

"He should have thought of that before he drew on me, Sheriff."

Grady pointed an accusatory finger at Clint.

"You told me you weren't lookin' for trouble."

"And I wasn't."

"What do you call this?"

"Trouble I wasn't looking for, that's for sure," Clint said. "It was Red McFall who went looking for trouble, not me."

"And you obliged him."

119

"All I was trying to do was keep him from hitting Brenda Tyler," Clint said. "He took it a step further and went for his gun. What was I supposed to do, let him shoot me?"

Grady opened his mouth to answer, and Clint cut him off.

"Don't answer that," he said. "I know him killing me would have caused you less heartache. Sorry I couldn't oblige."

Grady made a face and asked, "Are you pressin' charges against Red?"

"No," Clint said. "I'd have to stay around for a trial, and who knows how long that would take. No, I'm not pressing charges. If what the doctor says is true, he's going to pay for what he did for the rest of his life. That's good enough for me."

"Look," Grady said, "I don't wish you any ill, Adams, but now I have to deal with Pat McFall, and I'm not looking forward to it—and neither should you."

"Me?" Clint asked.

"That's right," Grady said. "Pat McFall is not gonna take this well, you shootin' his son."

"His son drew first."

Grady shook his head.

"That won't matter to McFall," Grady said. "You'll find that out pretty soon."

"How soon?"

"He should be here any minute," Grady said. "His spread is not that far away."

"Great," Clint said. "Just great."

"Thinkin' about leavin' town yet?" Grady asked hopefully.

"No."

Grady scowled and said, "I was afraid of that."

As if on cue, the door opened and a man stepped in, a tall, well-fed man in his fifties who looked a lot like Red McFall would look in about twenty years. Behind came a younger man, probably the other son.

"Sheriff," the man said, "what's this nonsense about my son bein' shot?"

Clint saw Grady flinch, but gave the man credit for holding his ground.

"It ain't nonsense, Mr. McFall," Grady said. "Red got into a scuffle, went for his gun, and got shot."

"Who shot him?"

Before Grady could answer, Clint said, "I did."

Pat McFall turned to face Clint head-on. The younger man stood just to his father's left and a step behind him, as if he'd been trained to do so.

"And who are you?"

"The name's Clint Adams."

"Pa," the other man said, "he's that gun-fighter—" Pat McFall held up his hand and his son immediately broke off what he was saying. Apparently, the younger son was very well trained.

"You're a professional gun hired by Nelson Fox," Pat McFall said.

"I don't hire my gun out, Mr. McFall."

"Is that a fact?"

"Yes, it is."

"Well, I'm callin' you a liar," McFall said. "Why else would you gun down my son?"

"I didn't gun him down, Mr. McFall," Clint said, "I defended myself. As for the reason I shot him, how about because he was a damn fool?"

McFall frowned and studied Clint with interest.

"What was this scuffle you and my son got into that resulted in a shootin'?"

"He was about to strike a woman."

"What woman?"

"Brenda Tyler."

McFall laughed derisively.

"My son wouldn't hit a woman, let alone Brenda," McFall said. "He wants to marry her."

"Well," Clint said, "if he had any chance at all of that, I think he took care of it today."

McFall firmed his jaw and said, "I say my son doesn't hit women."

"Right," Clint said, "he just beats them with his gun."

"What the hell does that mean?"

"Ask the sheriff," Clint said. "I'm tired of talking about this."

"Don't walk away from me, Adams," McFall demanded as Clint headed for the door.

At the door he turned and said, "That tone of voice might work with your hands, McFall, or with your sons, or maybe even with the Sheriff, but it doesn't work with me. I shot your son in self defense. Be grateful that he's not dead."

"Pa," the other man said, "you ain't gonna let him leave—"

"Shut up, Ben."

"But Pa," Ben McFall said, "he shot Red—"

"I said be still, boy!" McFall snapped, and Clint saw both the sheriff and Ben McFall flinch.

He'd had enough and left.

"Is what he said true?" Pat McFall asked the sheriff.

"Uh, which—"

"Did Red hit some woman?"

"Uh, well, Dorrie Washburn says that Red struck her—"

"Dorrie Washburn?" McFall repeated. "Do I know her?" He turned to his son and said, "Do I know her, Ben?"

"She's a widow who lives in town, Pa."

"Does Red know her?"

"I don't know, Pa."

"Where'd this happen, where is this supposed to have happened?" McFall asked.

"Over at Brenda's store," Grady said. "Seems Dorrie was tendin' to the business while Brenda was havin' dinner with the Foxes . . . and Clint Adams."

"Adams and Brenda, huh?" McFall said. "Seems like Red might have had some cause to do what he did."

"To hit a woman and try to kill a man?" Grady asked.

"Are you arrestin' my son, Sheriff?" Pat McFall asked coldly.

"Uh, well, no," Grady said, "Adams isn't gonna press charges."

"And this Dorrie Washburn?"

Grady frowned because he didn't like what he was going to say.

"It's her word against his, Mr. McFall," he said. "I don't think Mrs. Washburn wants to go to court with that."

McFall nodded shortly, as if satisfied with everything he had just heard.

"How is my son?"

Grady didn't want to answer that one.

"I guess you'd have to ask the doctor that, Mr. McFall," he said. "That's where Red is now."

"I'm goin' over to see him," McFall said. He started for the door, then turned and said to Grady, "This ain't over, Sheriff."

"What do you mean, Mr. McFall?"

"I mean Clint Adams and Nelson Fox are not gonna get away with this."

"But Adams said he wasn't workin' for Fox," Grady said. "In fact, they're friends—"

"That's good enough for me," McFall said. "Maybe Adams didn't hire his gun out, maybe he's just tryin' to help his friend. Either way he made a bad mistake when he shot my boy."

"What are you plannin' to do, Mr. McFall?" Grady asked, trying to sound very official.

"Whatever I do, Sheriff," McFall said, pointing a thick forefinger at the lawman, "I expect you to stay out of my way."

"I don't know if I'm gonna be able to do that," Grady said, with a lump in his throat. "After all, I am the sheriff."

"Don't go thinkin' that's a permanent position, Grady," McFall said, "and don't go thinkin' that it's a job worth dyin' for." He looked at his youngest son and said, "Come on, Ben."

A half hour after Pat McFall had left Grady's office, the lawman still had that damned lump in his throat.

THIRTY-TWO

The next few days were tense for a lot of people.

They were tense for Clint because he felt sure that Pat McFall was not just going to forget about the shooting of his son. Nelson Fox had assured him of that the day after the incident.

"Whether McFall thinks you work for me or you're doin' me a favor, he's not gonna forget, Clint," Fox said.

"I know, Nels."

"If you're gonna stay around, you're gonna have to watch your back real careful."

"Well," Clint said, "I am going to stay around awhile, and I'm used to watching my back."

"Yeah, well, I'd feel better if you had somebody else to watch your back," Fox said. "I can do it if you stay out here."

"I can't do that, Nels," Clint said. "That would be too much like hiding out."

"Well, then take Cord with you when you go into town," Fox said.

"I can't do that either," Clint said.

"Why not?"

"I don't want to get him killed."

"So you're just gonna wait for McFall to come after you?"

"He won't."

"What do you mean?"

"Not himself, anyway," Clint said. "He'll hire someone."

"Same thing," Fox said. "You're gonna wait for his man to come after you."

"Understand my position, Nels," Clint said. "If I leave town, it looks like I'm running. I do that and I'm an even bigger target than I am now, for the rest of my life. The same thing applies if I hide out. My only choice is to stay out in the open and deal with whatever comes."

"Is that the way you've had to live your life, Clint?" Fox asked.

"That's it, Nels."

Nelson Fox thought that over for a while, then shook his head.

"I got to hand it to you," he said. "I don't think I could live that way."

"You could," Clint said, "if you had no other choice. You would."

It was a tense time too for Nelson Fox and his family. If Pat McFall thought that Fox had hired Clint, or even just asked for his help, what would the man do in retaliation?

The whole family was waiting.

The tension spread to town as well.

Sheriff Jack Grady was waiting for a fuse to reach the powder. Something was going to happen, that was for sure, and he still had not decided what he would do. Side with Adams against the McFalls? What if Pat McFall came out on top? What would happen to him then? His job, or even his life, might be in danger.

And that lump in his throat still wouldn't go away.

Brenda Tyler was tense. She had taken a liking to Clint Adams and didn't want anything to happen to him. She was sure that the McFalls would retaliate for the shooting of Red McFall, which she felt responsible for. If she hadn't blown up at Red, he wouldn't have tried to hit her and Clint wouldn't have had to shoot him in self-defense.

She had tried to explain to Pat McFall what had happened, but he didn't want to hear it. Red was his son, and that was all he cared about. Unless, of course, she was willing to reconsider Red's many marriage proposals, which she was not.

But would that refusal be the ultimate reason Clint Adams was killed?

The tension even spread to the McFall ranch. Ben McFall was eager to go against Clint

Adams, himself, and was constantly reminding his father of this fact.

"He'd kill you without a second thought," Pat McFall told his youngest son.

"Then I'll take some men with me."

"How many?" Pat asked. "Five? Ten? Twenty?"

"As many as it takes."

"And you might get the job done," the elder McFall conceded, "but he'd probably kill you first. I can't take that chance."

"Pa," Ben said, "we can't let him get away with what he done to Red."

"And we ain't," Pat McFall said, "but we got to have the right man for the job."

"Like who?"

"That's what I've been tryin' to figure out," McFall said.

For days McFall sent telegrams out, looking for the right man. Each time he thought he had found someone, they either couldn't take the job or they didn't want to take the job when they heard it was Clint Adams, the Gunsmith.

What Pat McFall didn't know was that on the fourth day following the shooting the man he was looking for rode into town of his own accord.

When Stephen Robinson rode into North Bend his heart was beating fast. Somewhere in this town Clint Adams was waiting for him—providing he hadn't left already, of course.

He felt good, though. He felt too damned good for that to be the case. The air smelled sweeter than anywhere else he'd ever been, and he felt better than he'd ever felt. Even the people on the street looked better, the women prettier.

This was his time.

THIRTY-THREE

Clint rode into North Bend that afternoon with Will Cord, who insisted that he had some errands to run for his boss.

After they dismounted Clint said, "Well, go and run your errands."

"What are you gonna do?" Cord asked.

"I'm going over to the saloon for a drink, and then I think I'll find someplace to have lunch."

"I'm hungry too," Cord said. "I'll tag along."

"Will—"

"That is, if you don't mind."

"Will," Clint said again, "I have a target painted on my back."

"I'll walk alongside you."

Clint stared at the young man for a moment and then said, "Okay, come on."

To get to the saloon, Clint and Will had to walk past Brenda's store. Clint chose to do so by crossing the street.

"Trying to avoid someone?" Will asked.

"None of your business."

At that moment, however, Brenda happened to be looking out the front window, and she saw Clint walking across the street. She ran from the store, not bothering to lock the door behind her.

"Clint!" she called, rushing across the street.

"Uh-oh," Will said. "Caught."

"Go on to the saloon," Clint said. "I'll meet you there."

"Sure," Will said, and he walked away just as Brenda reached Clint. In fact, Will even touched the brim of his hat before he left.

"You've been avoiding me," Brenda accused.

"Yes, I have."

"Why?"

"You know why."

"I'm not afraid, Clint."

"Well, I am," he said. "I don't want to be the cause of you getting killed before we even get a chance to know each other."

"And are we?"

"Are we what?"

"Going to get a chance to know each other? Before you leave town?"

He stared at her for a moment before he said, "That depends on what you mean by getting to know each other."

"I think you know what I mean."

Clint frowned. Did she want to sleep with him, or really get to know him? If it was the former, they might have time for that, but if it was the latter there was no way he'd be in North Bend *that* long.

"I guess we'll have to wait and see."

"Yes," she said, "we will . . . if you don't get killed first."

"I'm not going to get killed."

"If you do, it will be all my fault."

He took her by the shoulders and said, "That's nonsense. I had a choice. I could have simply let Red hit you and kept out of it."

"No," she said, "you couldn't have."

He smiled.

"You're right, I couldn't, but it still wasn't your fault."

"You can say that—"

"Did you leave your store unattended?"

She turned quickly and looked across the street.

"Yes, I did," she said. "I wanted to make sure I caught you—"

"Well, you did," he said. "Now go back to your store, and I'll come by later to talk."

"Do you mean it?"

"Yes, I mean it," he said, dropping his hands from her shoulders. "Go on. I'll see you later."

"You better show up," she warned him.

"Go."

He watched her as she crossed the street and entered her store, and then he continued on to the saloon. He discovered that instead of going to the saloon to wait for him, Will Cord had simply walked down a few doorways and waited for him.

"What are you doing?" he asked.

"Just waiting," Will said. "I didn't want you to get lonely on the way to the saloon."

"Yeah, sure," Clint said. He wondered if sticking with him was Will's own idea, or if Fox had ordered the young man to. Either way it was Will's choice in the long run. He'd been hired on to break broncs, not watch Clint's back.

"Is the lady mad?"

"No, she's not mad," Clint said, "but I'll have to go and talk to her later."

He noticed that as they walked, Will Cord's eyes took in everything ahead of them and alongside them and even behind them. As a backup, the younger man seemed pretty good. Clint just hoped he was as good with a gun.

After registering at the hotel and dropping his gear in his room, Stephen Robinson went looking for two things: a beer and a woman. He found both of them at the North Bend Saloon.

In fact, there were no girls working the saloon because it was so early. Robinson asked the bartender what he could do for him in that department.

"I might be able to help you," the bartender said, rubbing his jaw. "What's your preference?"

"She's got to smell good," Robinson said, "I like a fragrant woman."

"I see," the bartender said. "Do you want a blonde, a brunette—"

"Whatever," Robinson said. "I've been on the trail awhile. I just want a woman who smells good and isn't too old."

Actually, the bartender only knew one woman who was willing to work in the daytime, and she happened to be blond.

"Go up the stairs, first door on the left," he told the man. "Sara. Tell her I sent you."

"I pay you or her?" Robinson asked.

"Pay her."

"You'll get your cut, huh?"

The bartender just smiled humorlessly.

"I'll take my beer with me," Robinson said, and went up the stairs.

Precisely ten seconds later Clint Adams and Will Cord entered the saloon.

THIRTY-FOUR

Clint bought two beers, and he and Will walked to a corner table in the all but empty saloon. There was only one other man in the place, sitting alone at a table by the door, unaware that one floor above, in bed with a woman named Sara, was the man who called himself the Canadian Gun, whose sole purpose for being in town was to kill Clint Adams, the Gunsmith.

"Are you tellin' me the truth?" Sara asked Stephen Robinson.

"Of course I am," Robinson said. "Why would I lie to you? To get you into bed?" He spread his arms to indicate that they were already in bed together.

"Well, I guess not," she said.

Sara Giles was a small woman in her twenties with perky breasts, and a perfectly formed ass. Robinson had been very pleased when she answered her door and let him in. He only

had to tell her the bartender had sent him.
In seconds, he was naked and in bed with her,
her head tucked between his legs, her lips and
tongue working eagerly on him, bringing him
to an almost rock-hard fullness. After that she
slithered into his lap and took him inside of
her. He was delighted to find that she was
very wet and slick. He entered her easily and
deeply.

She rode him that way for a short time and,
because he had been on the trail for a while,
he shot his load quickly.

"It doesn't always happen that way," he told
her immediately, "I've just been without for a
while."

"Are we finished?" she asked.

"Oh no, Sara," Robinson said, with a smile.
"We haven't even started yet. Just give me a
few minutes to get ready again."

It was during that few minutes that he told
her he was a gunman with a big reputation
from Canada who had come to this country to
kill the Gunsmith.

"I guess you wouldn't lie," she said, agree-
ing with his logic. "How are you gonna
kill him? You gonna shoot him in the
back?"

"Of course not," Robinson said. "I intend to
kill him in a fair fight."

"Are you that fast?" Sara asked.

"I am that fast, yes indeed," Robinson said
proudly.

"Wow," she said, "I'm in bed with somebody
who's gonna be a legend."

"I already am a legend in Canada," he said, wanting her to know that, "but this will spread my fame throughout the United States. I will be known as the fastest gun of all."

"Wow," she repeated.

"And now . . ." He pulled the sheet off of himself to show her that he was fully rigid once again.

"Wow . . ." she said again as she leaned over him so that her hair spread out over his crotch and he felt the warmth of her mouth engulf him. . . .

Downstairs Clint and Will worked on their beer while Clint tried to find out from the younger man what these errands he had to run were, that he could afford to sit in the saloon and do nothing.

"Okay," Will finally said, "so I don't have any errands. You need somebody to watch your back, Clint, and whether you like it or not, I'm the guy."

"Was this Nelson's idea?" Clint asked.

"No," Will said, "it was mine."

Clint studied the other man for a few moments, then said, "I appreciate it, Will."

"You're welcome. But don't try to talk me out of it. I can usually hit what I aim at with a gun, Clint, you know that."

True, Clint had seen Will shoot when they hunted together, but that was with a rifle. He didn't know how well he could do with a handgun. It was Clint's experience, however, that most men who could shoot one could shoot the other as well. It was rare that a man was good with only a rifle or a pistol.

"All right," Clint said. "Why don't we get some lunch, and then we'll head back to the ranch."

"First," Will reminded him, "you have to talk with Brenda for a while, remember?"

"Are you going to back me up," Clint asked, "and be my conscience?"

As Clint and Will left the saloon, Stephen Robinson was standing at the window of Sara's room, which overlooked the street. He stood in the window naked and opened it so the room would get a breeze. He and Sara had worked up quite a sweat this time.

He saw the two men leaving the saloon and thought nothing of it. Sara had told him that the saloon opened gaming tables in the evening, and that the place was usually packed. It was there he hoped to encounter Clint Adams and talk to him before challenging him.

There was, after all, probably something that could be learned from the man before he killed him.

THIRTY-FIVE

Stephen Robinson did not meet Clint Adams in the saloon that night. Clint decided not to go into town. He'd stayed longer than he had planned that day because he'd stopped to talk to Brenda before he left. By the time he was done with explanations—only some of which she accepted—he was more than ready to go back to the Fox ranch.

He also thought—and why hadn't this occurred to him some days ago?—that it was time to talk seriously to Nelson Fox about his feud with Pat McFall. He had been thinking that it was none of his business, but on second thought, it certainly was his business, since he had put a bullet into one of the McFalls.

So while Clint talked to Nelson Fox about the McFalls, one of the McFalls went into the North Bend Saloon and met Stephen Robinson, the Canadian Gun.

• • •

When Ben McFall walked into the North Bend Saloon that night, he was looking for a fight. He had enough anger pent up inside of him to power a steam engine. He was angry at Clint Adams for shooting his brother, Red. He was angry at his brother for getting himself shot, and he was angry at his father for not letting him go after Clint Adams.

Pat McFall knew how angry Ben was, so he hadn't allowed him to go into town alone. He'd sent three of his men with him and given them instructions that if anything happened to Ben, their jobs were on the line.

"Goddamned wet nurse job," one of them, a man called Garrett, muttered as they entered the saloon.

"Hey, we're gettin' paid and we ain't breakin' our backs," a second man, Anderson, said.

"Shut up, you guys," the last man, Chaplin, said. "Let's just do what we gotta do and keep little Ben from gettin' hurt."

The three men followed "little Ben" to the bar, where he ordered a beer for himself and ignored them. Chaplin, who had worked for Pat McFall the longest, ordered beers for the three of them.

Ben was standing with his back to the bar, looking around, hoping to see Clint Adams. Hell, he'd promised his father he wouldn't go looking for Adams, but if he ran into the man there wasn't anything his father could say about that, was there?

So Ben McFall watched the crowd of men in the saloon, while Chaplin, Anderson, and Garrett watched him like three hawks.

Upstairs Robinson finally tired of Sara and started to get dressed.

"God," she said, lying on her back across the bed with her head hanging off it so that she was looking at him upside down. "I never met a man who could do it so many times in one afternoon."

"Well, I'm getting hungry, or we wouldn't be finished even yet," he said, buckling on his gun.

"Oh, I have to get up and go to work," she said. "It sounds pretty busy down there."

He looked down at her hard little body, admiring it. He reached down and ran his hands over her hard breasts. The nipples immediately tightened, and she closed her eyes and moaned.

"How much would I have to pay to keep you up here waiting for me?"

Her eyes widened and she said, "Really?"

"Yes, really."

"Well," she said, biting her lush lower lip, "let me think. . . ."

"Why don't you just stay up here and think," he said, moving toward the door. "I trust you to find a fair price."

"What if one of the other girls downstairs appeals to you?"

"In that case," he said, opening the door, "I'd have to bring her up here to share the bed with us."

As he left, Sara rolled over, stared at the door, and said, "Wow!"

When Robinson got downstairs he saw that Sara's hearing had been very good. The North Bend Saloon was indeed very busy. He had to elbow his way across the room to the bar, and then use his elbows again to make a place for himself. In doing so he bumped into the arm of a young man, causing him to spill beer all over himself.

"Hey!" the young man shouted. "Goddamn! You clumsy shit."

"Hey, I'm sorry," Robinson said. "Tell you what. I'll buy you another one."

"I'm drenched."

"It's only beer, friend," Robinson said. "Take it easy."

"I'll take it easy," the man said, swinging his fist at Robinson.

Robinson nimbly took a step back and moved his chin, and the man's fist went flying by. In that same moment he saw three men who were standing behind the first, and they looked very concerned. He surmised that they were with the younger man, and that he might have to tangle with all four of them if he didn't do something to defuse the situation.

He had to show them who they were dealing with.

The young man regained his balance and whirled around. Robinson didn't know how much beer he'd had, but he couldn't take any chances.

"Stand still!" he shouted, but the man advanced on him again.

"Ben, don't!" somebody shouted.

Robinson watched as the young man's hand went for his gun, a painfully slow move. Robinson produced his gun as if by magic, not even his best move, but certainly enough to impress this bunch.

"You're painfully close to dying over some spilt beer, friend," Robinson said.

"Jeez," somebody said, "did you see how fast that was?"

"I saw it," another man said, "but I don't believe it."

Robinson sensed that it was the men with "Ben" who were speaking.

"Now calm down and let me buy you another beer," Robinson said, "and we can forget all about this."

Ben stared at Robinson for a few moments, then wiped the back of his hand across his mouth. Before he could say or do anything, though, one of the other men moved to his side and said something into his ear.

"Your father," Chaplin said to Ben, "is gonna want to meet this man."

THIRTY-SIX

Stephen Robinson could not believe his good luck. First, to find a woman like Sara, who was also a match for his sexual appetite. Lord, the woman was always ready for him! And then spilling beer on the son of a man who would not only find Clint Adams for him, but would pay him to kill him.

That kind of luck usually only came to the pure of heart.

What had he done to deserve it?

He met Ben McFall out in front of the hotel the following morning.

"Are you certain your father will pay me to do this?" Robinson asked.

"Oh, I'm sure," Ben said. "Remember, Adams shot my brother, and he works for Nelson Fox. With one shot Adams got his face into my father's private life and his business. Oh, yeah, Pa will pay you for this."

"Well, what do you think of that?" Robinson said. "I'm sure glad I didn't kill you last night, Ben."

"Yeah," Ben said sourly, "me too."

Nelson Fox had put Clint off the night before when he wanted to talk about business, and about Pat McFall. Now, the next morning, they were outside walking, just the two of them.

"Come on, Nels," Clint said, "I think it's time you talked to me."

"Maybe so," Fox said, "maybe so."

They walked a little further from the house, and Clint allowed his friend to work up to it.

"Business was good for a long time, Clint," he said finally, "and then Pat McFall came along. Now, when I say business was good, I don't mean I was getting rich. We were getting by, you know? Fixing the place up, hiring some hands. We were doing okay."

He fell silent, and Clint waited.

"Then McFall came along, and he was rich to start with, so right away when he started operating he had the best of everything. He took some of my business away, but that wasn't enough for him. We might have still been able to survive, but he decided that he didn't want any competition at all. He announced that he was going to grind my business into the dust, and he proceeded to do just that. I'm almost finished, Clint."

"Isn't there enough business for the both of you?" Clint asked.

"Probably," Fox said. "In fact, I even went to see McFall with the same thought, but he just laughed. He said if he couldn't have it all, then he didn't want any."

Clint nodded. He'd met a lot of men like Patrick McFall. Power hungry, only happy when they were grinding their boot heels into the back of somebody's neck. No wonder his son Red was the way he was.

"Do you want my help, Nelson?"

Fox didn't answer right away.

"I been invitin' you here for years, Clint," he said finally. "Most any other time you might have come, things would have been fine. You just happened to come when I'm havin' trouble with Donna, and with my business, and with . . ."

"Jeff?"

Fox glanced briefly at Clint, then looked away.

"Yeah," he said, "yeah, I'm havin' some problems with Jeff. It shows, huh?"

"Yes, Nels, it shows. What kind of problem are we talkin' about?"

"Oh, nothin' much," Fox said. "The boy seems to have got it into his head that I'm not his father."

"What?"

"Yeah," Fox said.

Clint scratched his chin.

"I don't know that I can help you with that, Nels," he said.

"Oh, I don't expect you to," Fox said. "If I need your help anywhere, it's with my business. I'll have to handle my family myself."

"Well, okay," Clint said. "How do I help you with your business?"

There was a long moment of silence and then Fox said, "I don't know, Clint. I just don't know."

"Well," Clint said, "maybe we can figure something out."

After leaving Fox, Clint went looking for Carol and found her out back, hanging clothes to dry.

"You come to help me with the laundry, Clint?" she asked.

"I want to ask you some questions, Carol," Clint said, "questions I might not have any right to ask."

She stopped what she was doing and turned to face him.

"You're our friend, Clint, and our guest," she said. "If you have any questions, you go ahead and ask them."

"Okay," he said, "okay . . ."

THIRTY-SEVEN

"Nice place," Stephen Robinson said. "Did your father build it?"

Ben McFall looked at Robinson and said, "His money built it."

Robinson and Ben McFall dismounted, and Ben called a hand over to take both horses.

"Pa's inside," Ben said.

"Lead on, young Ben."

Robinson followed him up the stairs to the large porch, where another man was sitting on a wooden bench covered with pillows. He was sitting to one side, leaning on his right hip.

"Red," Ben said, "what are you doing out here?"

"I'm goin' crazy inside," Red McFall said.

"Doesn't it still hurt?" Ben asked.

"Of course it hurts," Red snapped, "but I wanted to see this special gun you talked Pa into hiring to take care of Clint Adams."

"That would be me," Robinson said cheerfully. "I gather you are Red McFall, the one Mr. Adams shot in the hip?"

"That's right," McFall said. "You don't look like much to me."

"I saw his move, Red," Ben said. "He's fast."

"Well, I've seen Clint Adams's move," Red said, "so he better be fast."

"Oh," Robinson said, "I am."

"We'll see."

"Come inside, Stephen," Ben said. "Pa's waitin'."

"Yeah," Red said, "Pa's waitin'—with his wallet."

"The best part of a man," Robinson said, then followed Ben into the house.

Red McFall shifted his weight and winced as the pain lanced through his wounded hip. He was also suffering from mixed emotions. He wanted Clint Adams to pay for what he had done to him, but he wanted to be the one to make him pay. Also, he'd like to think that the fastest gun around had put a bullet into his hip, and the only way he'd be able to say that was if Adams outdrew this stranger from Canada.

And then there was the fact that Clint Adams was American, and Stephen Robinson was a foreigner.

Red McFall was nothing if not patriotic.

Ben McFall walked Stephen Robinson to his father's office, where Pat McFall was waiting.

McFall had listened patiently the night before while Ben described what had happened in the North Bend Saloon between him and the stranger.

"Where's he from?" McFall had asked.

"Canada."

"Canada?" McFall repeated in disbelief.

"That's right."

Pat McFall rubbed his jaw.

"You don't expect a fast gun to come out of Canada," McFall said.

"He's fast, Pa," Ben said. "Believe me, I know."

Pat McFall knew his son didn't have the experience to back that statement up, but so far he hadn't succeeded in finding someone to take on the job of handling Clint Adams. What was the harm in talking to this fella from Canada?

Now Pat McFall stood up behind his desk and studied the stranger standing next to his son. He was young, about Red's age, although not as formidable-looking as his elder son, but McFall knew that when it came to a gun in the hand, the way a man looked rarely had anything to do with it.

"So you fancy yourself a hand with a gun, eh, young fella?"

"If you're the businessman I think you are, Mr. McFall," Robinson said, "then you've already checked me out for yourself."

"As a matter of fact," McFall said, picking up a telegraph flimsy from his desk, and then another, "I have. I have some friends up near

the border who checked up on you for me in
Canada." He held one telegram up. "Then I
have some information on your exploits since
you entered this country. Apparently you are
fairly good with a gun, as you claim."

"I don't claim to be fairly good, Mr. McFall,
I claim to be the best."

"Yes, well, many men have claimed that,
haven't they?" McFall asked. "And they
were proven wrong—all but Clint Adams, of
course."

"I understand from your son that you would
be willing to pay to have Adams killed."

"That's correct."

"Because he shot your son?"

"And because he is working for my competi-
tor."

"I want you to understand," Robinson said,
"that I came here specifically to kill Clint
Adams. No one was paying me."

"Well, I'll pay you," McFall said, "and I don't
care how you do it."

"There is only one way I will do it," Robinson
said, "and that will be face-to-face."

"Well, if that's your intention," McFall said,
"I'll pay you after the job is done."

Robinson smiled and said, "That's fine. And
now, as to the terms . . ."

THIRTY-EIGHT

"I was married before," Carol told Clint. "It was a bad marriage, and it ended badly."

"I didn't know that."

"No one did," she said. "Soon after that I met Nelson, and I knew he was the man I should have been with all along. We got married quickly, and Jeff was born soon after that."

Clint waited, but there was no more coming. They were still standing out among the hanging clothes and Carol was staring at them.

"Carol?"

"All right, yes," she said, "yes, Jeff's father was my first husband, not Nelson."

Clint was surprised.

"How could Jeff know that?"

"I don't know," she said. "I think he just . . . feels it."

"Where is his father?"

"Dead."

"How?"

She looked at him then, tears shining in her eyes.

"I killed him."

Now he was really stunned.

"He used to get drunk and beat me. One night he came home drunk and started beating on me. Donna came in, and he started to yell at her, and he hit her. I was willing to put up with him hitting me, but not Donna." She paused a moment, took a deep breath, and said, "Right then and there I got a knife and stuck it in him." She wiped away a tear with an angry swipe of her hand. "That's what I meant when I said the marriage ended badly."

"So Nelson has been Jeff's father since the day he was born."

"Yes," she said, "and he's been a wonderful father."

"Does Nels know?"

She smiled, but there was no humor in it, just irony.

"Nelson swept me off my feet, Clint," she said, "and we married so soon that when I told him I was pregnant he didn't bother with math. He just accepted that the baby was his."

Clint frowned. Nelson Fox—the Nelson Fox he knew—was smarter than that. He wondered if there just wasn't too much silence going on here. If Nelson and Carol talked, maybe Nelson would tell her that he knew and didn't care. If they would all talk—Nelson, Carol, and Jeff—maybe the whole thing could be ironed out.

"You can't tell either one of them, Clint," she said, suddenly desperate. "You can't."

"Carol . . . why did you tell me?"

"You asked me."

"And Nelson never has?"

"No," she said. She smiled again, now a smile of friendship. She put her hand on his arm and said, "I guess I've been wanting to tell someone all these years and you were the lucky one."

Suddenly she put her head against his chest and he held her for a few moments before she pulled away.

"I have to finish the laundry."

"One more question."

"Okay."

"What about Donna? She knows that Nelson is not her father, doesn't she?"

"She's accepted Nelson as her father, and she swore to me she would never tell Jeff."

"Do you think she's kept the promise?" Clint asked.

"Oh yes," she said with certainty, "I'm sure she hasn't told him. She wouldn't."

"Not even in a moment of anger?"

She shook her head.

"My children get along well, Clint," she said. "They love each other. She'd never tell him because she knows it would hurt him."

"You'll excuse me for saying this, Carol," he said, "but it seems to be the *not* knowing that's hurting both him and Nelson now."

She thought about that for a moment, then hugged herself and said, "I have to finish the laundry."

"All right," he said. "Thanks for talking to me."

For just a moment he wanted to ask her about the business, but he decided he'd brought her enough grief for one afternoon.

"I'll see you later," he said, and left her to her laundry.

As he came around to the front of the house, he saw Jeff coming out and instinctively ducked back out of sight. As he watched the boy walk to the stable, he laughed to himself and shook his head. It was funny the way knowing a secret affected you. There really was no reason he should avoid Jeff, but as soon as he saw him his first thought was to avoid him.

Secrets. He'd never liked them. He thought they were especially dangerous in families— and this was a perfect example.

This family seemed to have a lot of secrets from each other. Was it his business to try and bring them out into the open?

While he was mulling that over, he noticed riders approaching, three of them. As they got closer he recognized two of them. The third was a stranger.

"Company comin'?" Nelson asked, walking over from the corral.

"I don't think you're going to consider these people company, Nels."

THIRTY-NINE

Nelson Fox came over to stand shoulder to shoulder with Clint. As the riders got closer, Jeff came out of the barn.

"Jeff!" Fox shouted. "Get over here, quick!"

Jeff responded to the urgency in Fox's voice and rushed over to stand with his father and Clint.

"Should I get a rifle, Pa?"

"Just stand still, Jeff, and don't say anything," Clint said. "I get the feeling these men are here to see me and not your father." To Fox Clint said, "Do you know the other man?"

"No," Fox said, "never saw him before."

"Well," Clint said, "we'll find out who he is soon enough."

As the three men rode up on them, they reined in their horses and stared down at Clint, Fox, and Jeff. Three against three, Clint found himself thinking, but the odds were not in their favor since Nelson Fox and Jeff were not armed.

"Morning, Fox," Pat McFall said.

He was the man in center, flanked by his son Ben and the other man.

"What do you want, McFall?" Fox demanded.

"Is that any tone of voice to use with a neighbor?" the man asked.

Clint saw McFall's eyes flick past them and knew that Carol must have come around from the side of the house.

"Morning, ma'am," McFall said.

Nelson turned and saw Carol, but Clint kept his eyes on the three men—especially the unknown man. He didn't know who the man was, but he was fairly sure what he was. It was in the cocky way he sat his horse and the arrogant gleam in his eyes.

"There ain't a neighborly bone in your body, McFall," Fox said. "Spit out what you want and get off my land."

"I just came by to introduce my new man," McFall said. "I thought Adams here might want to meet him."

"Oh?" Clint asked. "And why's that?"

"Well, you and him seem to have a lot in common."

"I don't think I have anything in common with this man," Clint said.

"And why would you say that, Mr. Adams?" Stephen Robinson asked. "You don't even know me."

"I know your type, friend."

"My type?" Robinson repeated, laughing. "And what type would that be, sir?"

"The type that usually ends up doing something foolish."

"Is that a fact?" the man asked. "Well, let me introduce myself anyway. My name is Stephen Robinson, and I've come a long way to do two things."

"And what would they be?" Clint asked.

"Well, one of them was to meet you," Robinson said.

"And the other?"

"Why, to kill you."

Clint heard Carol's sharp intake of breath behind him.

"Where are you from, Robinson, that you came such a long way?"

"Canada."

"Do you have a reputation there?"

"Oh, yes," Robinson said. "I'm called the Canadian Gun. Actually, there was nothing left for me to prove in Canada, so I had to come here and try the best."

"I'm flattered."

"As you should be," Robinson said, with supreme arrogance.

Clint had been called out many times before by men of all ages and attitudes but rarely had he ever genuinely disliked them.

In the span of five minutes, Stephen Robinson had managed to accomplish that.

"So you're hiring your gun out?" Clint asked.

"Actually," Robinson said, "I came here to kill you for free, just for my own satisfaction."

"And now you're going to take money for it."

"I'll answer that," Patrick McFall said. "I don't hire men for their guns, and I sure don't hire men to kill. Mr. Robinson is simply my new hand."

"What do you know about horses, Robinson?" Clint asked.

Robinson laughed and said, "I know how to ride them, that's about all."

"Good choice for a new hand, McFall," Nelson Fox said. "Congratulations."

"Well," McFall said, ignoring the jibe, "I just wanted my new man to meet your new man."

"Clint Adams doesn't work for me," Nelson Fox said. "He happens to be a friend of the family."

"Well," McFall said, "whatever. Whether he works for you or is a friend, he made a mistake when he shot my boy, Red."

"That was explained to you," Fox said.

"Sure," McFall said, "by Adams, and by Red. Who do you think I believe?"

"Believe who you want," Nelson Fox said, "but get off my land."

"I'll get off your land, Fox," McFall said, "but I have the feeling it's not going to be your land much longer."

Before Nelson Fox could say anything, Donna Fox came from the other side of the house and stopped when she saw all the people. Alongside of her was Will Cord.

"Hello, Donna," Ben McFall called out.

"Stay there, Donna," Fox called out.

"My son was only saying hello to her, Fox," McFall said.

"I don't want your son anywhere near her, or talking to her, McFall."

"My son's not good enough for your daughter?" McFall demanded.

"Not nearly, McFall."

The two older men glared at each other, and then McFall jerked on his horse's reins, turning it.

Ben McFall threw one last lovesick look at Donna Fox and followed his father.

"See you soon, Adams," Robinson said.

"I'll watch my back."

Robinson bristled at those words and seemed to lose some of his composure.

"When I come for you, Mr. Gunsmith, it will be face-to-face," he said coldly. "You can depend on that."

"I'll look forward to it."

"I wouldn't," Robinson said, and turned his horse to follow his new employer.

FORTY

"Have you ever heard of this Canadian Gun?" Nelson asked Clint.

"No, never."

"Can you take him?"

"Clint can take anyone," Jeff said.

"That's not true, Jeff," Clint said.

"What?"

"I won't know who's better until the time comes," Clint explained. "None of us will."

"But . . . nobody's faster than you are."

"Nobody has been," Clint said, "up till now."

"If you're not sure," Carol said, coming up next to them, "then why face him? Why not just leave?"

Clint looked at Nelson Fox, who said, "I'll explain it to her, Clint."

"I have to ride into town," Clint said.

"What for?" Fox asked.

"Talk to the sheriff," Clint said, "see what he knows about this Canadian Gun."

"But—" Carol started.

"Let's go inside and talk, Carol," Fox said.

162

"Clint?" Jeff asked. "Can I come with you?"

"You better stay here, Jeff," Clint said, "close to home."

"I'll go with you," Will Cord said, coming up behind them.

"Will!" Donna said.

"Go inside with your father, Donna," Cord said to her.

Nelson Fox looked from his daughter to Cord and back again, puzzled.

"Clint?" Cord said.

"All right, Will," Clint said, "come ahead."

"Will!" Donna said, her tone plaintive.

"Donna!" Cord said back to her. His tone was a warning. She was acting improper in front of her father.

"Donna," Nelson Fox said from the porch, "come inside."

Donna turned and looked at Will, but it was Clint who spoke so that her mother and father couldn't hear him.

"Go on inside, Donna."

"You be careful, Will Cord," she said, and turned and ran into the house.

Cord watched her go, then turned to Clint and said, "I might be in trouble here. My job, I mean."

"Nels Fox is not . . . unreasonable, Will."

"Men and their daughters, Clint," Cord said. "I've had this problem before."

"That's because every woman," Clint said, "was somebody's daughter, Will. Are we going to town?"

Cord nodded. "Let's go."

FORTY-ONE

When Clint and Cord got to town, they rode directly to the sheriff's office. Sheriff Jack Grady was not happy to see them when they entered.

"Do you know about this gunman Patrick McFall has hired?" Clint asked without preamble.

Grady stood up and walked to his coffeepot. He concentrated on pouring himself a cup.

"I know about it."

"What are you going to do about it?"

"What can I do?" Grady asked. "Mr. McFall has hired himself a new hand. That's not against the law."

"He's hired a man to kill me," Clint said.

"I don't know that."

"Oh yes," Clint said, "you do know that, Sheriff. You know that as well as I do."

"You can't prove it."

"No," Clint said, "I can't—not until he comes after me. What do you expect me to do when that happens?"

Grady finally turned around and looked at Clint. The cup of coffee in his hand was trembling.

"You'll do what you have to do," he said. "That's between you and McFall, or you and the gunman . . . whatever his name is."

"Robinson," Clint said, "Stephen Robinson. Calls himself the Canadian Gun."

"I never heard of him," Grady said. He gestured with his hands and spilled coffee onto the floor and over his hand, wrist, and arm. "Shit."

"I never heard of him, either," Clint said, and then added more to himself then to Grady or Cord, "but maybe I know someone who has."

"Who?" Grady asked.

Instead of answering Clint said to Cord, "Let's go, Will."

"Where?"

"I want to send a telegram."

As Clint and Cord left the office, Grady called out, "Who do you mean?"

Outside, as they walked to the telegraph office, Cord asked, "Who *do* you mean?"

"A friend of mine," Clint said, "a friend of mine with a lot of connections."

FORTY-TWO

At the telegraph office Clint sent a telegram to his friend, Rick Hartman, in Labyrinth, Texas, with a very simple question: WHO THE HELL IS THE CANADIAN GUN?

"Is he gonna understand that?" Will Cord asked, looking over Clint's shoulder.

"If he has heard of him, he'll understand and give us some information," Clint said, handing the message to the clerk to turn into a telegram. "If he hasn't, it won't mean anything anyway."

"Are we gonna wait for an answer?"

"Yes," Clint said, "but not here. Come on, I'll buy you a beer."

They walked over to the Cactus Hall Saloon, and when they got there Cord said, "My turn to buy."

"Okay," Clint said. "Beer."

He took a corner table and waited for Cord to come over with two mugs of beer. Only two other tables were occupied at this time of the afternoon.

"So is this what it's like to be you?" Cord asked.

Clint was sipping his beer at the time, and he choked at the question.

"What do you mean?"

"I mean, sitting around waiting for some-body to try to kill you?"

"No," Clint said, "it's not what my life is like."

"But sometimes?"

"Yes," Clint said, "sometimes."

They sat in silence then until Clint said, "You got any more dumb questions?"

"Well . . . yeah, I do," Cord said. "What do I tell Mr. Fox when I get back to the ranch?"

"About what?"

"He's gonna ask me what's goin' on between me and Donna," Cord said. "What should I tell him?"

"How about the truth?"

"That we've been sleepin' together?"

"Well, no," Clint said, "not that truth. Do you love her?"

Cord made a face.

"She keeps askin' me that."

"Well, maybe it's time to come up with an answer," Clint said.

"I guess."

At that moment a door in the back opened and Bruce Stilwell, the owner of the saloon, came out. When he saw Clint, he hurriedly walked over to his table.

"Did you pay for those beers?" he asked Clint.

Will Cord looked taken aback.

"*I* paid for them," he said. "Ask the bartender."

"No, no, you don't understand," Stilwell said. Then he turned to Clint and said, "From now on, you don't pay for drinks here."

"Why not?" Clint asked.

"Because you've given me a chance to make a lot of money, Adams."

"How do you figure that?"

"I'm taking bets on you and that fella, Stephen Robinson."

"You're what?"

"That's right," Stilwell said. "You know, there are actually people willing to bet on him just because he's younger? Of course, I am giving odds."

"You're taking bets on who lives and who dies?" Clint asked the saloon owner.

"Well, yeah," Stilwell said. "Isn't that the biggest gamble of all? Living or dying?"

Clint stared at the man for a few moments, then realized that he couldn't argue with that.

"You're right, Stilwell," he said finally, "you're absolutely right." He drank his beer down, the one Cord had paid for, then pushed the empty mug toward Stilwell and said, "I'll have another."

FORTY-THREE

"I want it done today," Pat McFall told Robinson, "and I want it done in town. I want everyone to see what happens to anyone who hurts me or mine, or who tries to get in my way."

Robinson stared across McFall's desk at him.

"Well, there's a happy coincidence," he said. "I want to do it in town too. I want everyone to see me beat the fastest gun in the country."

"My son will go with you."

"And why would young Ben be going with me?" Robinson asked.

"To be my eyes," McFall said. "Ben and a man called Chaplin will accompany you."

"They won't interfere, will they?"

"No," McFall lied, "they won't interfere."

Ben McFall was very pleased with the instructions his father had given him a few moments ago.

"Don't do anything until Adams and Robinson have drawn. When that happens I want you and Chaplin to finish the job."

"You don't think Robinson will take Adams, Pa?" Ben asked.

"I don't know, son," McFall said, "but this is an opportunity that's too good to pass up. At the very least Robinson will keep Adams's attention."

"And what if Robinson does beat him?"

"Then don't do anything," McFall said. "Nothing, do you hear?"

"I hear ya, Pa."

"Don't take any chances, Ben. Is that clear?"

"It's clear, Pa."

Now Ben was waiting outside on the porch for Robinson to come out. Red McFall was sitting outside once again.

"So this is gonna be it, huh, little brother?"

"One way or another, Red," Ben said, "Adams is gonna pay today."

At that moment the front door opened and Stephen Robinson stepped out.

"Well, lookee here," Red McFall said, "the Canadian Gun himself."

"You know, Red," Robinson said, standing next to the younger brother and staring down at the older one, "I might have to change that name after I've killed the Gunsmith."

"*If* you kill him," Red said.

"I don't think in ifs, Red," Robinson said. "That shows doubt. I don't have any doubt about my ability. I will kill Clint Adams."

"That's fine," Red said. "Then I suppose I'll be seeing you back here later today."

"No doubt."

"Yeah."

Robinson turned and went down the steps.

"Hey, Ben?"

"Yeah, Red?"

"You be careful, huh?"

"Sure, Red."

"And do me a favor, will ya?"

"What?"

"After Adams kills this clown, go over to the saloon and collect my bet from Stilwell, okay?"

"You bet on Adams?"

"That's right."

"Bad bet, big brother," Ben said, shaking his head, "bad bet," and he went down the steps after Robinson.

FORTY-FOUR

They each had one more free beer and then left the saloon. They had just stepped outside when the telegraph clerk came running over.

"I have your answer, Mr. Adams."

"Good, thanks," Clint said, accepting the telegram.

The man, small, slender, and bespectacled, remained there instead of walking away.

"Didn't I pay you?" Clint asked, staring at the man.

"Yes, sir, you did."

"Is there something else I can do for you?"

"Well . . . I was wondering, Mr. Adams . . . I mean, I'm thinking about betting, and I was wondering if you could tell me—"

Cord stepped between Clint and the telegraph clerk and snapped at the man, "Get out of here!"

The man flinched, then turned and ran back to his office.

Cord turned to Clint and asked, "What's the telegram say?"

Clint, who had already scanned it, handed it to the younger man.

"He's never heard of him," Cord said, reading the telegram.

"I guess we're just going to have to find out who he is, and how good he is, when the time comes, Will," Clint said.

"And when do you think that will be?"

"Oh, I don't think it will be long," Clint said, "I don't think it will be long at all."

Clint was looking past Cord, who turned to see what he was looking at. Riding toward them down the center of the main street was Stephen Robinson, flanked by Ben McFall and another man. Patrick McFall was nowhere to be seen.

"He brought company," Cord said.

"I see that."

"Think they'll stay out of it?"

"I don't know," Clint said.

"I don't think they will."

Clint scratched his chin.

"Why don't you find yourself a spot to watch from, Will?"

"Okay."

As Clint watched the three men continue down the street toward him, Bruce Stilwell came outside.

"Oh, damn," Stilwell said. "Is it gonna happen now?"

"Maybe."

"It's too soon," the saloon owner complained. "I haven't taken enough bets."

"That's too bad."

"Do you think you could put him off for a few more days, Adams?"

Clint looked at Stilwell with distaste.

"What do you think the odds are, Stilwell," Clint asked, "that you could make it back into the saloon before I put a bullet in your foot?"

"You wouldn't."

"Want to bet?" Clint asked.

Stilwell matched Clint's stare for a few moments, then shook his head and said, "No."

He turned and went back into the saloon.

Clint stepped down into the street to await the arrival of the Canadian Gun.

"Stop right here," Robinson said to Ben McFall and Chaplin.

"What are we stopping for?" Chaplin asked.

"I'll go the rest of the way alone."

"What are we supposed to do?" Chaplin asked.

Robinson looked at him and said, "Find a place to watch from—and stay out of it."

"I don't want no part of this," Chaplin said.

"Keep it that way."

As Robinson rode ahead, Ben said, "Stand in front of that store over there and be ready. I'll be on the other side of the street."

"Yeah, sure," the man said.

"Don't mess this up, Chaplin," Ben said. "My pa wouldn't like it."

"I hear ya," Chaplin said, and they went to opposite sides of the street.

They were about thirty yards from where Clint Adams had just stepped into the street. This also put them level with Brenda Tyler's store. As she looked out her window, she saw the three men stopped in the street and recognized Ben McFall. She moved right against the window for a closer look. At that moment Will Cord entered her store.

"What's going on?" she asked.

"Just listen. . . ."

Clint watched as Robinson rode toward him without the other two men. They stayed where they were for a few moments then rode to opposite sides of the street. It would be hard to watch both of them and Robinson. He had to hope that Robinson was telling the truth about wanting to face him one-on-one.

FORTY-FIVE

"Good afternoon, Mr. Adams," Robinson said. "Or may I call you Clint?"

"You can call me Mr. Adams."

Robinson laughed. "You have a sense of humor," he said. "I find that . . . interesting. You know, I had hoped that we could talk before we . . . clashed."

"Clashed?" Clint repeated. "Is that what you call it?"

"For want of a better word," Robinson said. "Can we talk for a while?"

"About what?"

"There are some . . . things that I could probably learn from you."

This time Clint laughed.

"What good would that do you, Robinson?" he asked. "You'd have to be alive to use what you learned."

Robinson regarded Clint for a moment, still looking down from astride his horse.

"You're confident," he said. "That's good."

"I have some advice for you, Robinson."

"And what would that be, Mr. Adams?"

"While you're still on your horse," Clint said, "why don't you ride out of town?"

Robinson smirked, dismounted, and stood facing Clint.

"Now I'm not on my horse," he said. He tied the animal off to a nearby post and turned to face Clint again.

"It's time," he said.

"Your arrogance is amazing."

"You call it arrogance," Robinson said, "I call it confidence."

Clint looked around and suddenly he was aware that they were being watched, from windows, doors, from around corners, they were being watched probably by half the town—and probably half of them had bet on the outcome.

"We're putting on a show here, Robinson," he said. "Look around. Is this what you want?"

Robinson did look around and said, "This is exactly what I want."

Clint looked at the man, shook his head, and said, "Let's get out into the street, then."

So here it was, after all this time, Stephen Robinson thought. Just what he had been waiting for. The whole town watching and Clint Adams standing right in front of him, ready to help make his dream come true.

"Whenever you're ready," he told Clint Adams.

"Whatever you say," Clint replied.

Robinson watched Clint . . . and watched . . . and watched . . . and still the man did not go for his gun. He was used to moving only after his opponent moved.

Why didn't Adams draw?

Ah, Robinson thought then, he's waiting for me. He doesn't want to make the first move. Well, then, that was all right with him. He didn't have all day to wait anyway.

Swiftly—faster than he had ever moved before—he went for his gun, felt the butt in his hand, and started to draw it, keeping his eyes on Clint, waiting for the Gunsmith to go for his gun.

Suddenly Clint Adams's gun was in his hand, and Robinson still hadn't pulled his gun from his holster.

It couldn't be.

"Wait—" he mouthed, but it was too late.

Clint Adams fired.

Ben McFall watched from his position in a store doorway, and when Stephen Robinson started to fall he put his hand down to draw his gun. Before he could, however, he felt the cold barrel of someone else's gun press against the side of his neck.

"Don't do it, Ben," Will Cord said. "Don't even think about it."

Across the street Chaplin sighed as he saw Robinson fall. It was no surprise to him. He'd never been impressed by the man. With no enthusiasm at all he drew his gun, but before he could aim it at Clint Adams, Brenda Tyler swung a shovel from inside her store. It crashed through her window and smashed into the back of Chaplin's head, felling him before he even knew what hit him.

Clint heard the sound of breaking glass and looked up the street. He saw Will Cord marching Ben McFall toward him at gunpoint. From across the street Brenda Tyler was running toward him with a large shovel in her hands. It wasn't hard for him to figure out what the breaking glass had been.

Will Cord reached him first and looked down at Stephen Robinson's body, which Clint was standing next to.

"Hey, what do ya know," Cord said, "I won my bet."

FORTY-SIX

Brenda's body was long and lean. She had pale, creamy skin that made the brown of her nipples seem even darker.

"This," she had said, while undressing for him next to her bed, "is what I call getting to know each other better. Since you're leaving soon, I decided to take matters into my own hands."

It was the day after the shooting, and Clint had already decided that it was time to leave. He had said good-bye to Nelson Fox and his family, and now he was saying good-bye to Brenda—or he thought he was. She had invited him upstairs and had locked up her store to take him there.

"I don't think I can help you with your business problems, Nels," he had told Nelson Fox the night before. "Actually I think I should get out of your way so you can take care of them yourself."

"I understand," Nelson Fox said. "If I end up losing the business, Clint, Carol and me and the kids will just have to go on to something else."

"You'll make it, Nels," Clint said, "but I have one piece of advice for you."

"What's that?"

"Talk with your family more," Clint said. "There are things you should all be telling each other."

"You're right," Fox said. "I've already talked to Donna and Will, and I know you're right."

He'd said good-bye to Jeff, and Donna, and Carol, giving her the same advice he'd given her husband.

She hugged him and said, "Telling you has helped me. I think now maybe I can talk to them about it."

"Good," he said, "then I did help."

She kissed his cheek and said, "More than you know, Clint."

After Brenda undressed for him, she helped him to undress. By the time she finished removing his clothes, he had a raging erection that she took in her hand and used to lead him to the bed.

"I was leaving town today," he said breathlessly as she continued to run her pussy over him. The feel of her wiry pubic hair on his penis was amazing.

"You'll just have to leave tomorrow."

"Tomorrow?" he asked. "You mean to keep me in this bed all day?"

She lifted her hips, and when she came down this time she engulfed him, taking him into her wet, steamy depths.

"Do you have any objections?"

"Just a question."

"What?"

He groaned as she moved on him and asked, "What are the odds that I'll come out of this alive?"

"It would be better if you asked," she replied breathlessly as she rode him, "if you're going to *want* to leave after today. . . ."

Watch for

SEMINOLE VENGEANCE

157th in the exciting GUNSMITH series
from Jove!

Coming in January!

*If you enjoyed this book,
subscribe now and get...*

TWO FREE

A $7.00 VALUE–

If you would like to read more of the very best, most exciting, adventurous, action-packed Westerns being published today, you'll want to subscribe to True Value's Western Home Subscription Service.

Each month the editors of True Value will select the 6 very best Westerns from America's leading publishers for special readers like you. You'll be able to preview these new titles as soon as they are published, *FREE* for ten days with no obligation!

TWO FREE BOOKS

When you subscribe, we'll send you your first month's shipment of the newest and best 6 Westerns for you to preview. With your first shipment, two of these books will be yours as our introductory gift to you absolutely *FREE* (a $7.00 value), regardless of what you decide to do. If

you like them, as much as we think you will, keep all six books but pay for just 4 at the low subscriber rate of just $2.75 each. If you decide to return them, keep 2 of the titles as our gift. No obligation.

Special Subscriber Savings

When you become a True Value subscriber you'll save money several ways. First, all regular monthly selections will be billed at the low subscriber price of just $2.75 each. That's at least a savings of $4.50 each month below the publishers price. Second, there is never any shipping, handling or other hidden charges—*Free home delivery*. What's more there is no minimum number of books you must buy, you may return any selection for full credit and you can cancel your subscription at any time. A TRUE VALUE!